Sarah Johnson Prichard

The Only Woman in the Town

And Other Tales of the American Revolution

Sarah Johnson Prichard

The Only Woman in the Town
And Other Tales of the American Revolution

ISBN/EAN: 9783337023126

Printed in Europe, USA, Canada, Australia, Japan

Cover: Foto ©Andreas Hilbeck / pixelio.de

More available books at **www.hansebooks.com**

THE OLD PORTER HOUSE.
In it were sheltered and cared for many soldiers in
the War of the Revolution

The Only Woman in the Town

And Other Tales of the
..American Revolution..

BY

SARAH J. PRICHARD

Author of the History of Waterbury, 1674-1783

PUBLISHED BY
MELICENT PORTER CHAPTER
DAUGHTERS OF THE AMERICAN REVOLUTION
WATERBURY, CONN.
1898

PREFACE

The celebration of the Centennial Anniversary of the United States at the city of Philadelphia in 1876, and the exhibit there made of that nation's wonderful growth and progress, gave a new and remarkable impulse to the germs of patriotism in American life. The following tales of the American Revolution— with the exception of the last—were written twenty-two years ago, and are the outcome of an interest then awakened. They all appeared in magazines and other publications of that period, from which they have been gathered into this volume, in the hope that thereby patriotism may grow stronger in the children of to-day.

CONTENTS

————

THE ONLY WOMAN IN THE TOWN.

NE hundred years and one ago, in Boston, at ten of the clock one April night, a church steeple had been climbed and a lantern hung out.

At ten, the same night, in mid-river of the Charles, oarsmen two, with passenger silent and grim, had seen the signal light out-swung, and rowed with speed for the Charlestown shore.

At eleven, the moon was risen, and the grim passenger, Paul Revere, had ridden up the Neck, encountered a foe, who opposed his ride into the country, and, after a brief delay, had gone on, leaving a British officer lying in a clay pit.

At midnight, a hundred ears had heard the flying horseman cry, "Up and arm. The Regulars are coming out!"

You know the story well. You have heard how the wild alarm ran from voice to voice and echoed beneath every roof, until the men of Lexington and Concord were stirred and aroused with patriotic fear for the safety of the public stores that had been committed to their keeping.

You know how, long ere the chill April day began to dawn, they had drawn, by horse power and by hand power, the cherished stores into

2

safe hiding-places in the depth of friendly forest-coverts.

There is one thing about that day that you have *not* heard and I will tell you now.   It is, how one little woman staid in the town of Concord, whence all the women save her had fled.

All the houses that were standing then, are very old-fashioned now, but there was one dwelling-place on Concord Common that was old-fashioned even then!   It was the abode of Martha Moulton and " Uncle John."   Just who " Uncle John " was, is not known to the writer, but he was probably Martha Moulton's uncle.   The uncle, it appears by record, was eighty-five years old; while the niece was *only* three-score and eleven.

Once and again that morning, a friendly hand had pulled the latch-string at Martha Moulton's kitchen entrance and offered to convey herself and treasures away, but, to either proffer, she had said : " No, I must stay until Uncle John gets the cricks out of his back, if all the British soldiers in the land march into town. "

At last, came Joe Devins, a lad of fifteen years—Joe's two astonished eyes peered for a moment into Martha Moulton's kitchen, and then eyes and owner dashed into the room, to learn what the sight he there saw could mean.

" Whew ! Mother Moulton, what are you doing ?"

" I'm getting Uncle John his breakfast to be

sure, Joe," she answered. "Have *you* seen so many sights this morning that you don't know breakfast, when you see it? Have a care there, for hot fat *will* burn," as she deftly poured the contents of a pan, fresh from the fire, into a dish.

Hungry Joe had been astir since the first drum had beat to arms at two of the clock. He gave one glance at the boiling cream and the slices of crisp pork swimming in it, as he gasped forth the words, "Getting breakfast in Concord *this* morning! *Mother Moulton*, you *must* be crazy."

"So they tell me," she said, serenely. "There comes Uncle John!" she added, as the clatter of a staff on the stone steps of the stairway outrang, for an instant, the cries of hurrying and confusion that filled the air of the street.

"Don't you know, Mother Moulton," Joe went on to say, "that every single woman and child have been carried off, where the Britishers won't find 'em?"

"I don't believe the king's troops have stirred out of Boston," she replied, going to the door leading to the stone staircase, to open it for Uncle John.

"Don't believe it?" and Joe looked, as he echoed the words, as though only a boy could feel sufficient disgust at such a want of common sense, in full view of the fact, that Reuben Brown had just brought the news that eight men had been killed by the king's Red Coats in Lexington, which fact he made haste to impart.

" I won't believe a word of it," she said, stoutly,
" until I see the soldiers coming."

"Ah! Hear that!" cried Joe, tossing back his
hair and swinging his arms triumphantly at an
airy foe. " You won't have to wait long. *That
signal* is for the minute men. They are going to
march out to meet the Red Coats. Wish I was a
minute man, this minute."

Meanwhile, poor Uncle John was getting down
the steps of the stairway, with many a grimace
and groan. As he touched the floor, Joe, his face
beaming with excitement and enthusiasm, sprang
to place a chair for him at the table, saying,
" Good morning," at the same moment.

" May be," groaned Uncle John, " youngsters
like you may think it is a good morning, but *I don't.*
Such a din and clatter as the fools have kept up all
night long. If I had the power" (and now the
poor old man fairly groaned with rage), " I'd make
'em quiet long enough to let an old man get a wink
of sleep, when the rheumatism lets go."

" I'm real sorry for you," said Joe, " but you
don't know the news. The king's troops, from
camp, in Boston, are marching right down here,
to carry off all our arms that they can find.

"Are they?" was the sarcastic rejoinder. " It's
the best news I've heard in a long while. Wish
they had my arms, this minute. They wouldn't
carry them a step further than they could help, I
know. Run and tell them that mine are ready,
Joe."

"But, Uncle John, wait until after breakfast, you'll want to use them once more," said Martha Moulton, trying to help him into a chair that Joe had placed on the white sanded floor.

Meanwhile, Joe Devins had ears for all the sounds that penetrated the kitchen from out of doors, and he had eyes for the slices of well-browned pork and the golden-hued Johnny-cake lying before the glowing coals on the broad hearth.

As the little woman bent to take up the breakfast, Joe, intent on doing some kindness for her in the way of saving treasures, asked, "Sha'n't I help you, Mother Moulton?"

"I reckon I am not so old that I can't lift a mite of corn-bread," she replied with chilling severity.

"Oh, I didn't mean to lift *that thing,*" he made haste to explain, "but to carry off things and hide 'em away, as everybody else has been doing half the night. I know a first-rate place up in the woods. Used to be a honey tree, you know, and it's just as hollow as anything. Silver spoons and things would be just as safe in it—" but Joe's words were interrupted by unusual tumult on the street and he ran off to learn the news, intending to return and get the breakfast that had been offered to him.

Presently he rushed back to the house with cheeks aflame and eyes ablaze with excitement. "They're coming!" he cried. "They're in sight down by the rocks. They see 'em marching, the men on the hill do!"

"You don't mean that it's really true that the soldiers are coming here, *right into our town!*" cried Martha Moulton, rising in haste and bringing together, with rapid flourishes to right and to left, every fragment of silver on it. Divining her intent, Uncle John strove to hold fast his individual spoon, but she twitched it without ceremony out from his rheumatic old fingers, and ran next to the parlor cupboard, wherein lay her movable treasures.

"What in the world shall I do with them?" she cried, returning with her apron well filled, and borne down by the weight thereof.

"Give 'em to me," cried Joe. "Here's a basket. Drop 'em in, and I'll run like a brush-fire through the town and across the old bridge, and hide 'em as safe as a weasel's nap."

Joe's fingers were creamy; his mouth was half filled with Johnny-cake, and his pocket on the right bulged to its utmost capacity with the same, as he held forth the basket; but the little woman was afraid to trust him, as she had been afraid to trust her neighbors.

"No! No!" she replied, to his repeated offers. "I know what I'll do. You, Joe Devins, stay right where you are until I come back, and, don't you even *look* out of the window."

"Dear, dear me!" she cried, flushed and anxious when she was out of sight of Uncle John and Joe. I *wish* I'd given 'em to Colonel Barrett when he was here before daylight, only, I *was* afraid I should never get sight of them again.

She drew off one of her stockings, filled it, tied the opening at the top with a string—plunged stocking and all into a pail full of water and proceeded to pour the contents into the well.

Just as the dark circle had closed over the blue stocking, Joe Devins' face peered down the depths by her side, and his voice sounded out the words: "O Mother Moulton, the British will search the wells the *very* first thing. Of course, they *expect* to find things in wells!"

"Why didn't you tell me before, Joe? but now it is too late."

"I would, if I had known what you was going to do; they'd been a sight safer in the honey tree."

"Yes, and what a fool I've been—flung *my watch* into the well with the spoons!"

"Well, well! Don't stand there, looking!" as she hovered over the high curb, with her hand on the bucket. Everybody will know, if you do."

"Martha! Martha!" shrieked Uncle John's quavering voice from the house door.

"Bless my heart!" she exclaimed, hurrying back over the stones.

"What's the matter with your heart?" questioned Joe.

"Nothing. I was thinking of Uncle John's money," she answered.

"Has he got money?" cried Joe. "I thought

he was poor, and you took care of him because
you were so good !"

Not one word that Joe uttered did the little
woman hear. She was already by Uncle John's
side and asking him for the key to his strong box.

Uncle John's rheumatism was terribly exasper-
ating. " No, I won't give it to you!" he cried,
" and nobody shall have it as long as I am above
ground."

" Then the soldiers will carry it off," she said.

" Let 'em !" was his reply, grasping his staff
firmly with both hands and gleaming defiance out
of his wide, pale eyes. "*You* won't get the key,
even if they do."

At this instant, a voice at the doorway shouted
the words, " Hide, hide away somewhere, Mother
Moulton, for the Red Coats are in sight this minute !"

She heard the warning, and giving one glance
at Uncle John, which look was answered by
another "No, you won't have it," she grasped
Joe Devins by the collar of his jacket and thrust
him before her up the staircase so quickly that
the boy had no chance to speak, until she released
her hold, on the second floor, at the entrance to
Uncle John's room.

The idea of being taken a prisoner in such a
manner, and by a woman, too, was too much for
the lad's endurance. " Let me go !" he cried,
the instant he could recover his breath. " I won't
hide away in your garret, like a woman, I won't.

I want to see the militia and the minute men fight the troops, I do."

"Help me first, Joe. Here, quick now! Let's get this box out and up garret. We'll hide it under the corn and it'll be safe," she coaxed.

The box was under Uncle John's bed.

"What's in the old thing anyhow?" questioned Joe, pulling with all his strength at it.

The box, or chest, was painted red, and was bound about by massive iron bands.

"I've never seen the inside of it," said Mother Moulton. "It holds the poor old soul's sole treasure, and I *do* want to save it for him if I can."

They had drawn it with much hard endeavor as far as the garret stairs, but their united strength failed to lift it. "Heave it, now!" cried Joe, and lo! it was up two steps. So they turned it over and over with many a thudding thump;—every one of which thumps Uncle John heard and believed to be strokes upon the box itself to burst it asunder —until it was fairly shelved on the garret floor.

In the very midst of the overturnings, a voice from below had been heard crying out, "Let my box alone! Don't you break it open! If you do, I'll—I'll—" but, whatever the poor man *meant* to threaten as a penalty, he could not think of anything half severe enough to say, so left it uncertain as to the punishment that might be looked for.

"Poor old soul!" ejaculated the little woman, her soft white curls in disorder and the pink color rising from her cheeks to her fair forehead, as she

bent to help Joe drag the **box** beneath the rafter's
edge.

" Now, Joe, " she said, " we'll **heap** nubbins
over it, and if the soldiers want corn **they**'ll take
good ears **and never** think **of touching poor**
nubbins. So they fell to work **throwing corn over
the** red chest, until it was completely **concealed**
from view.

Then Joe **sprang to** the high-up-window **ledge in**
the point **of** the roof and took one glance **out.**
" Oh, I see them, **the** Red Coats ! 'Strue's I live,
there go **our** militia *up the hill.* I thought they
was going **to stand and** defend. Shame on 'em, I
say!" Jumping down **and crying back** to Mother
Moulton, " **I'm going to stand by the** minute
men, " **he went down,** three steps **at a leap,** and
nearly overturned **Uncle** John **on the stairs, who,**
with many groans, was trying to get **to the** defense
of his strong box.

" What **did** you help **her for, you scamp ?**" he
demanded of Joe, flourishing his staff **unpleasantly**
near the **lad's** head.

"'Cause she asked me **to,** and **couldn't do it
alone,**" returned Joe, dodging the **stick and**
disappearing from the scene at the very moment
Martha Moulton **encountered Uncle J**ohn.

" Your strong **box is safe** under nubbins in the
garret, unless the house burns **down, and** now that
you are up here, you had **better stay,**" she added
soothingly, as she hastened **by him to** reach the
kitchen below.

Once there, she paused a second or two to take resolution regarding her next act. She knew full well that there was not one second to spare, and yet she stood looking, apparently, into the glowing embers on the hearth. She was flushed and excited, both by the unwonted toil and the coming events. Cobwebs from the rafters had fallen on her hair and homespun dress, and would readily have betrayed her late occupation to any discerning soldier of the king.

A smile broke suddenly over her fair face, displacing for a brief second every trace of care. "It's my old weapon, and I must use it," she said, making a stately courtesy to an imaginary guest, and straightway disappeared within an adjoining room. With buttoned door and dropped curtains the little woman made haste to array herself in her finest raiment. In five minutes she reappeared in the kitchen, a picture pleasant to look at. In all New England, there could not be a more beautiful little old lady than Martha Moulton was that day. Her hair was guiltless now of cobwebs, but haloed her face with fluffy little curls of silvery whiteness, above which, like a crown, was a little cap of dotted muslin, pure as snow. Her erect figure, not a particle of the hard-working-day in it now, carried well the folds of a sheeny, black silk gown, over which she had tied an apron as spotless as the cap.

As she fastened back her gown and hurried away the signs of the breakfast she had not eaten, the clear pink tints seemed to come out with added beauty of coloring in her cheeks, while her hair seemed fairer and whiter than at any moment in her three-score and eleven years.

Once more, Joe Devins looked in. As he caught a glimpse of the picture she made, he paused to cry out: "All dressed up to meet the robbers! My, how fine you do look! I wouldn't. I'd go and hide behind the nubbins. They'll be here in less than five minutes now," he cried, "and I'm going over the North Bridge to see what's going on there."

"O Joe, stay, won't you?" she urged, but the lad was gone, and she was left alone to meet the foe, comforting herself with the thought, "They'll treat me with more respect if I *look* respectable, and if I *must* die, I'll die good-looking in my best clothes, anyhow."

She threw a few sticks of hickory-wood on the embers and then drew out the little round stand, on which the family Bible was always lying. Recollecting that the British soldiers probably belonged to the Church of England, she hurried away to fetch Uncle John's "prayer book."

"They'll have respect to me, if they find me reading that, I know," she thought. Having drawn the round stand within sight of the well, and where she could also command a view of the staircase, she sat and waited for coming events.

Uncle John was keeping watch of the advancing troops from an upper window. "Martha," he

called, "you'd better come up. They're close
by, now." To tell the truth, Uncle John himself
was a little afraid; that is to say, he hadn't quite
courage enough to go down and, perhaps, encounter his own rheumatism and the king's soldiers on
the same stairway, and yet, he felt that he must
defend Martha as well as he could.

The rap of a musket, quick and ringing, on the
front door, startled the little woman from her
apparent devotions. She did not move at the
call of anything so profane. It was the custom of
the time to have the front door divided into two
parts, the lower half and the upper half. The for-
mer was closed and made fast, the upper could be
swung open at will.

The soldier getting no reply, and doubtless
thinking that the house was deserted, leaped over
the chained lower half of the door.

At the clang of his bayonet against the brass
trimmings, Martha Moulton groaned in spirit, for,
if there was any one thing that she deemed essen-
tial to her comfort in this life, it was to keep spotless, speckless and in every way unharmed, the
great knocker on her front door.

"Good, sound English metal, too," she thought,
"that an English soldier ought to know how to
respect."

As she heard the tramp of coming feet she only
bent the closer over the Book of Prayer that lay
open on her knee. Not one word did she read or
see; she was inwardly trembling and outwardly

watching the well and the staircase. But now, above all other sounds, broke the noise of Uncle John's staff thrashing the upper step of the staircase, and the shrill, tremulous cry of the old man, defiant, doing his utmost for the defense of his castle.

The fingers that lay beneath the book tingled with desire to box the old man's ears, for the policy he was pursuing would be fatal to the treasure in garret and in well; but she was forced to silence and inactivity.

As the king's troops, Major Pitcairn at their head, reached the open door and saw the old lady, they paused. What could they do but look, for a moment, at the unexpected sight that met their view: a placid old lady in black silk and dotted muslin, with all the sweet solemnity of morning devotion hovering about the tidy apartment and seeming to centre at the round stand by which she sat,—this pretty woman, with pink and white face surmounted with fleecy little curls and crinkles and wisps of floating whiteness, who looked up to meet their gaze with such innocent, prayer-suffused eyes.

"Good morning, Mother," said Major Pitcairn, raising his hat.

"Good morning, gentlemen and soldiers," returned Martha Moulton. "You will pardon my not meeting you at the door, when you see that I was occupied in rendering service to the Lord of all." She reverently closed the book, laid it on the table, and arose, with a stately bearing, to demand their wishes.

"We're hungry, good woman," spoke the commander," and your hearth is the only hospitable one we've seen since we left Boston. With your good leave I'll take a bit of this, and he stooped to lift up the Johnny-cake that had been all this while on the hearth.

"I wish I had something better to offer you," she said, making haste to fetch plates and knives from the corner-cupboard, and all the while she was keeping eye-guard over the well. "I'm afraid the Concorders haven't left much for you to-day," she added, with a soft sigh of regret, as though she really felt sorry that such brave men and good soldiers had fallen on hard times in the ancient town. At the moment she had brought forth bread and baked beans, and was putting them on the table, a voice rang into the room, causing every eye to turn toward Uncle John. He had gotten down the stairs without uttering one audible groan, and was standing, one step above the floor of the room, brandishing and whirling his staff about in a manner to cause even rheumatism to flee the place, while at the top of his voice he cried out:

"Martha Moulton, how *dare* you *feed* these— these—monsters—in human form?"

"Don't mind him, gentlemen, *please* don't," she made haste to say; "he's old, *very* old; eighty-five, his last birthday, and—a little hoity-toity at times," pointing deftly with her finger in the region of the reasoning powers in her own shapely head.

Summoning Major Pitcairn by an offer of a dish of beans, she contrived to say, under cover of it:

"You see, sir, I couldn't go away and leave him; he is almost distracted with rheumatism, and this excitement to-day will kill him, I'm afraid."

Advancing toward the staircase with bold and soldierly front, Major Pitcairn said to Uncle John:

"Stand aside, old man, and we'll hold you harmless."

"I don't believe you will, you red-trimmed trooper, you," was the reply; and, with a dexterous swing of the wooden staff, he mowed off and down three military hats.

Before any one had time to speak, Martha Moulton, adroitly stooping, as though to recover Major Pitcairn's hat, which had rolled to her feet, swung the stairway-door into its place with a resounding bang, and followed up that achievement with a swift turn of two large wooden buttons, one high up, and the other low down, on the door.

"There!" she said, "he is safe out of mischief for a while, and your heads are safe as well. Pardon a poor old man, who does not know what he is about."

"He seems to know remarkably well," exclaimed an officer.

Meanwhile, behind the strong door, Uncle John's wrath knew no bounds. In his frantic endeavors to burst the fastenings of the wooden buttons, rheumatic cramps seized him and carried the day, leaving him out of the battle. .

Meanwhile, a company of soldiers clustered about the door. The king's horses were fed within five feet of the great brass knocker, while, within the house, the beautiful little old woman, in her Sunday-best-raiment, tried to do the dismal honors of the day to the foes of her country. Watching her, one would have thought she was entertaining heroes returned from the achievement of valiant deeds, whereas, in her own heart, she knew full well that she was giving a little, to save much.

Nothing could exceed the seeming alacrity with which she fetched water from the well for the officers : and, when Major Pitcairn gallantly ordered his men to do the service, the little soul was in alarm ; she was so afraid that "somehow, in some way or another, the blue stocking would get hitched on to the bucket." She knew that she must to its rescue, and so she bravely acknowledged herself to have taken a vow (when, she did not say), to draw all the water that was taken from that well.

" A remnant of witchcraft ! " remarked a soldier within hearing.

"Do I look like a witch?" she demanded.

"If you do," replied Major Pitcairn, "I admire

3

New England witches, and never would condemn one to be hung, or burned, or—smothered."

Martha Moulton never wore so brilliant a color on her aged cheeks as at that moment. She felt bitter shame at the ruse she had attempted, but silver spoons were precious, and, to escape the smile that went around at Major Pitcairn's words, she was only too glad to go again to the well and dip slowly the high, over-hanging sweep into the cool, clear, dark depth below.

During this time the cold, frosty morning spent itself into the brilliant, shining noon.

You know what happened at Concord on that 19th of April in the year 1775. You have been told the story—how the men of Acton met and resisted the king's troops at the old North Bridge; how brave Captain Davis and minute-man Hosmer fell; how the sound of their falling struck down to the very heart of mother earth, and caused her to send forth her brave sons to cry "Liberty, or Death!"

And the rest of the story; the sixty or more barrels of flour that the king's troops found and struck the heads from, leaving the flour in condition to be gathered again at nightfall, the arms and powder that they destroyed, the houses they burned; all these, are they not recorded in every child's history in the land?

While these things were going on, for a brief while, at mid-day, Martha Moulton found her home deserted. She had not forgotten poor, suffering, irate Uncle John in the regions above, and so, the very minute she had the chance, she made a strong cup of catnip tea (the real tea, you know, was brewing in Boston harbor).

She turned the buttons, and, with a bit of trembling at her heart, such as she had not felt all day, she ventured up the stairs, bearing the steaming peace-offering before her.

Uncle John was writhing under the sharp thorns and twinges of his old enemy, and in no frame of mind to receive any overtures in the shape of catnip tea; nevertheless, he was watching, as well as he was able, the motions of the enemy. As she drew near, he cried out:

"Look out this window, and see! Much *good* all your scheming will do *you!*"

She obeyed his command to look, and the sight she then saw caused her to let fall the cup of catnip tea and rush down the stairs, wringing her hands as she went, and crying out:

"Oh, dear! what shall I do? The house will burn and the box up garret. Everything's lost!"

Major Pitcairn, at that moment, was on the green in front of her door, giving orders.

Forgetting the dignified part she intended to play; forgetting everything but the supreme danger that was hovering in mid-air over her home—the old house wherein she had been born, and the only home she had ever known—she rushed out upon the green, amid the troops and surrounded by cavalry, and made her way to Major Pitcairn.

" The court-house is on fire ! " she cried, laying
her hand upon the commander's arm.

He turned and looked at her.   Major Pitcairn
had recently learned that the task he had been
set to do in the provincial towns that day was not
an easy one; that, when hard pressed and trodden down, the despised rustics, in home-spun
dress, could sting even English soldiers ; and thus
it happened that, when he felt the touch of
Mother Moulton's plump little old fingers on his
military sleeve, he was not in the pleasant humor
that he had been when the same hand had ministered to his hunger in the early morning.

" Well, what of it? *Let it burn!* We won't
hurt *you*, if you go in the house and stay there ! "

She turned and glanced up at the court-house.
Already flames were issuing from it. " Go in the
house and let it burn, *indeed !* " thought she.
" He knows *me*, don't he? Oh, sir! for the love
of Heaven won't you stop it?" she said, entreat-
ingly.

" Run in the house, good mother. That is a
wise woman," he advised.

Down in her heart, and as the very outcome of
lip and brain she wanted to say, " You needn't
' mother ' me, you murderous rascals ! " but, remembering everything that was at stake, she
crushed her wrath and buttoned it in as closely as
she had Uncle John behind the door in the morning, and again, with swift gentleness, laid her
hand on his arm.

He turned and looked at her. Vexed at her persistence, and extremely annoyed at intelligence that had just reached him from the North Bridge, he said, imperiously, "Get away! or you'll be trodden down by the horses!"

"I *can't* go!" she cried, clasping his arm, and fairly clinging to it in her frenzy of excitement. "Oh, stop the fire, quick, quick! or my house will burn!"

"I have no time to put out your fires," he said, carelessly, shaking loose from her hold and turning to meet a messenger with news.

Poor little woman! What could she do? The wind was rising, and the fire grew. Flame was creeping out in a little blue curl in a new place, under the rafter's edge, *and nobody cared.* That was what increased the pressing misery of it all. It was so unlike a common country alarm, where everybody rushed up and down the streets, crying "Fire! fire! f-i-r-e!" and went hurrying to and fro for pails of water to help put it out.

Until that moment the little woman did not know how utterly deserted she was.

In very despair, she ran to her house, seized two pails, filled them with greater haste than she had ever drawn water before, and, regardless of Uncle John's imprecations, carried them forth, one in either hand, the water dripping carelessly down the side breadths of her fair silk gown, her silvery curls tossed and tumbled in white confusion, her pleasant face aflame with eagerness, and her clear eyes suffused with tears.

Thus equipped with facts and feeling, she once more appeared to Major Pitcairn.

"Have you a mother in old England?" she cried. "If so, for her sake, stop this fire."

Her words touched his heart.

"And if I do —?" he answered.

"*Then your johnny-cake on my hearth won't burn up,*" she said, with a quick little smile, adjusting her cap.

Major Pitcairn laughed, and two soldiers, at his command, seized the pails and made haste to the court-house, followed by many more.

For awhile the fire seemed victorious, but, by brave effort, it was finally overcome, and the court-house saved.

At a distance Joe Devins had noticed the smoke hovering like a little cloud, then sailing away still more like a cloud over the town; and he had made haste to the scene, arriving in time to venture on the roof, and do good service there.

After the fire was extinguished, he thought of Martha Moulton, and he could not help feeling a bit guilty at the consciousness that he had gone off and left her alone.

Going to the house he found her entertaining the king's troopers with the best food her humble store afforded.

She was so charmed with herself, and so utterly well pleased with the success of her pleading, that the little woman's nerves fairly quivered with jubilation; and best of all, the blue stocking was still safe in the well, for had she not watched with her own eyes every time the bucket was dipped to fetch up water for the fire, having, somehow, got rid of the vow she had taken regarding the drawing of the water.

As she saw the lad looking, with surprised countenance, into the room where the feast was going on, a fear crept up her own face and darted out from her eyes. It was, lest Joe Devins should spoil it all by ill-timed words.

She made haste to meet him, basket in hand.

"Here, Joe," she said, "fetch me some small wood, there's a good boy."

As she gave him the basket she was just in time to stop the rejoinder that was issuing from his lips.

In time to intercept his return she was at the wood-pile.

"Joe," she said, half-abashed before the truth that shone in the boy's eyes—"Joe," she repeated, "you know Major Pitcairn ordered the fire put out, *to please me*, because I begged him so, and, in return, what *can* I do but give them something to eat? Come and help me."

"I won't," responded he. "Their hands are red with blood. They've killed two men at the bridge."

"Who's killed?" she asked, trembling, but Joe would not tell her. He demanded to know what had been done with Uncle John.

"He's quiet enough, up-stairs," she replied,

with a sudden spasm of feeling that she *had* neg-
lected Uncle John shamefully ; still, with the day,
and the fire and everything, how could she help
it? but, really, it did seem strange that he made
no noise, with a hundred armed men coming and
going through the house.

At least, that was what Joe thought, and, having deposited the basket of wood on the threshold
of the kitchen door, he departed around the corner of the house. Presently he had climbed a pear
tree, dropped from one of its overhanging
branches on the lean-to, raised a sash and crept
into the window.

Slipping off his shoes, heavy with spring mud,
he proceeded to search for Uncle John. He was
not in his own room ; he was not in the guest-
chamber ; he was not in any one of the rooms.

On the floor, by the window in the hall, looking out upon the green, he found the broken cup
and saucer that Martha Moulton had let fall.
Having made a second round, in which he inves-
tigated every closet and penetrated into the
spaces under beds, Joe thought of the garret.

Tramp, tramp went the heavy feet on the
sanded floors below, drowning every possible
sound from above ; nevertheless, as the lad opened
the door leading into the garret, he whispered
cautiously : "Uncle John! Uncle John!"

All was silent above. Joe went up, and was
startled by a groan. He had to stand a few
seconds, to let the darkness grow into light, ere

he could see; and, when he could discern out-
lines in the dimness, there was given to him the
picture of Uncle John, lying helpless amid and
upon the nubbins that had been piled over his
strong box.

"Why, Uncle John, are you dead?" asked Joe,
climbing over to his side.

"Is the house afire?" was the response.

"House afire? No! The confounded Red
Coats up and put it out."

"I thought they was going to let me burn to
death up here!" groaned Uncle John.

"Can I help you up?" and Joe proffered two
strong hands, rather black with toil and smoke.

"No, no! You can't help me. If the house
isn't afire, I'll stand it till the fellows are gone,
and then, Joe, you fetch the doctor as quick as
you can."

"*You* can't get a doctor for love nor money this
night, Uncle John. There's too much work to be
done in Lexington and Concord to-night for
wounded and dying men; and there'll be more of
'em too afore a single Red Coat sees Boston again.
They'll be hunted down every step of the way.
They've killed Captain Davis, from Acton."

"You don't say so!"

"Yes, they have, and —"

"I say, Joe Devins, go down and do—do something. There's *my niece* a-feeding the murderers!
I'll disown her. She shan't have a penny of my
pounds, she shan't!"

Both Joe and Uncle John were compelled to remain in inaction, while below, the weary little woman acted the kind hostess to His Majesty's troops.

But now the feast was spent, and the soldiers were summoned to begin their painful march. Assembled on the green, all was ready, when Major Pitcairn, remembering the little woman who had ministered to his wants, returned to the house to say farewell.

'Twas but a step to her door, and but a moment since he had left it, but he found her crying; crying with joy, in the very chair where he had found her at prayers in the morning.

" I would like to say good-by," he said; "you've been very kind to me to-day."

With a quick dash or two of the dotted white apron (spotless no longer) to her eye, she arose. Major Pitcairn extended his hand, but she folded her own closely together, and said:

" I wish you a pleasant journey back to Boston, sir."

" Will you not shake hands with me before I go?"

" I can feed the enemy of my country, but shake hands with him, *never!*"

For the first time that day the little woman's love of country seemed to rise triumphant within her, and drown every impulse to selfishness; or, was it the nearness to safety that she felt? Human conduct is the result of so many motives that it is sometimes impossible to name the compound, although on that occasion Martha Moulton labelled it "Patriotism."

"And yet I put out the fire for you," he said.

"For your mother's sake, in old England, it was, you remember, sir."

"I remember," said Major Pitcairn, with a sigh, as he turned away.

"And for *her* sake I will shake hands with you," said Martha Moulton.

So he turned back, and, across the threshold, in presence of the waiting troops, the commander of the expedition to Concord and the only woman in the town shook hands at parting.

Martha Moulton saw Major Pitcairn mount his horse; heard the order given for the march to begin—the march of which you all have heard. You know what a sorry time the Red Coats had of it in getting back to Boston; how they were fought at every inch of the way, and waylaid from behind every convenient tree-trunk, and shot at from tree-tops, and aimed at from upper windows, and besieged from behind stone walls, and, in short, made so miserable and harassed and overworn, that at last their depleted ranks, with the tongues of the men parched and hanging, were fain to lie down by the road-side and take what came next, even though it might be death. And then *the dead* they left behind them!

Ah! there's nothing wholesome to mind or body about war, until long, long after it is over

and the earth has had time to hide the blood, and
send forth its sweet blooms of Liberty.

The men of that day are long dead. The same
soil holds regulars and minute-men. England,
which over-ruled, and the provinces, that put out
brave hands to seize their rights, are good friends
to-day, and have shaken hands over many a
threshold of hearty thought and kind deed since
that time.

The tree of Liberty grows yet, stately and fair,
for the men of the Revolution planted it well, and
surely, God himself *hath* given it increase. So we
gather to-day, in this our story, a forget-me-not
more, from the old town of Concord.

When the troops had marched away, the weary
little woman laid aside her silken gown, resumed
her homespun dress, and immediately began to
think of getting Uncle John down-stairs again
into his easy chair; but it required more aid than
she could give, to lift the fallen man. At last, Joe
Devins summoned returning neighbors, who came
to the rescue, and the poor nubbins were left to
the rats once more.

Joe climbed down the well and rescued the
blue stocking, with its treasures unharmed, even
to the precious watch, which watch was Martha
Moulton's chief treasure, and one of the very few
in the town.

Martha Moulton was the heroine of the day.
The house was besieged by admiring men and
women that night and for two or three days there-

after; but when, years later, she being older, and poorer, even to want, petitioned the General Court for a reward for the service she rendered in persuading Major Pitcairn to save the court-house from burning, there was granted to her only fifteen dollars, a poor little grant, it is true, but *just enough* to carry her story down the years, whereas, but for that, it might never have been wafted up and down the land, on the wings of this story.

A WINDHAM LAMB IN BOSTON TOWN.

T was one hundred and one years ago in this very month of June, that nine men of the old town of Windham— which lies near the northeast corner of Connecticut—met at the meeting-house door. There was no service that day; the doors were shut, and the bell in the steeple gave no sound.

The town of Windham had appointed the nine men a committee to ask the inhabitants to give from their flocks of sheep as many as they could for the hungry men and women of Boston. Each man of the committee was told at the meeting-house door the district in which he was to gather sheep.

On his stout grey pony sat Ebenezer Devotion. As soon as he heard the eastern portion of the town assigned to him, he gave the signal to his horse, and in five minutes was out of sight over the high hill. In ten minutes he was near the famous Frog pond. As he was passing it by, a voice from the marsh along its bank cried out:

" Where now, so fast, this fine morning, Mr. Devotion ? "

" The same to you, Goodwife Elderkin. I know your voice, though I can't see your face."

Presently a hand parted the thicket and a woman's face appeared.

" I'm getting flag-root. It gives a twang to root beer that nothing else will, and the flag hereabout is the twangiest I know of. Stop at the house as you go along and get some beer, won't you? Mary Ann's to home."

" Thank you," said Mr. Devotion, with a stiff bow. " It's a little early for beer this morning. I'll stop as I come this way again. How are your sheep and lambs this year?"

" First rate. Never better."

" Have you any to part with?"

" Who wants to buy?" and Goodwife Elderkin came out from the thicket to the road-side, eager for gain.

" We don't sell sheep in Windham this year," said Mr. Devotion.

" Why, what's the matter with the man?" thought Mrs. Elderkin, for Ebenezer Devotion liked to drive a good bargain as well as any one of his neighbors. Before she had time to give expression to her surprise, he said with a sharp inclination of his head toward the sun, " We've neighbors over yonder, good and true, who wouldn't sell sheep if we were shut in by ships of war, and hungry, too."

" What! any news from Boston town?"

" It's twenty-four days, to-day, since the port was shut up.'

Goodwife Elderkin laughed. Ebenezer Devotion looked grim enough to smother every bit of laughter in New England.

"'Pears as if king and Parliament really believed that tea was cast away by the men of Boston, now don't it? 'stead of every man, woman and child in the country havin' a hand in it," said Mrs. Elderkin.

" About the sheep!" replied Mr. Devotion, jerking up his horse's head from the sweet, pure grass, greening all the road-side.

" Let your pony feed while he can," she replied. " What about the sheep ?"

" How many will you give?"

" How many are you going to give yourself?"

" Twice as many as you will."

" Do you mean it?"

" I do."

" Then I'll give every sheep I own."

" And how many is that ?"

" A couple of dozen or so."

" Better keep some of them for another time."

Mrs. Elderkin laughed again. " I'll say half a dozen then, if a dozen is all you want to give yourself."

Ebenezer Devotion drew from his wallet a slip of paper and headed his list of names with " Six sheep, from Goodwife Elderkin."

" Thank you in the name of God Almighty and the country," he said, solemnly, as he jerked his pony's head from the grass and rode on.

Mrs. Elderkin watched him as he wound along

the pond-side and was lost to sight; then she, chuckling forth the words, " I knew well enough my sheep were safe," went back to the marsh after flag-root.

When every neighbor feels it a duty to carry intelligence from the last speaker he has met to the next hearer he may meet, news flies fast, so Goodwife Elderkin was prepared for the accost of Mr. Devotion. She did not linger long in the swamp, but, washing her hands free from mud in the water of the pond, walked swiftly home. By the time she reached her house, the gray pony and his rider were two miles away on the road to Canterbury. The cry of hunger and possible starvation in the town of Boston was spreading from village to village and from house to house.

Do you know how Boston is situated? It would be an island but for the narrow neck of land on the south side. On the east, west and north are the waters of Massachusetts Bay and Charles River. Just north from it, and divided only by the same river, is another almost island, with its neck stretched toward the north; and this latter place is Charlestown and contains Bunker's Hill. Not far from the two towns, in the bay, are many islands. Noddle's Island, Hog, Snake, Deer, Apple, Bird and Spectacle Islands are of the number. On these islands were many sheep and cattle, likewise hay and wood, all of which the inhabitants of Boston needed for daily

4

use, but by the Boston port bill, which went into
operation on the first day of June, no person was
permitted to land anything at either Boston or
Charlestown; and so the neck of Charlestown
reached out to the north for food and help, and
the neck of Boston pleaded with the south for
sustenance, and it was in answer to this cry that
our nine men of Windham went sheep-gathering.

The work went on for four days, and at the end
of that time 257 sheep had been freely given. The
owners drove them, on the evening of the 27th
day of the month, to the appointed place, and,
very early in the morning of the 28th, many of
the inhabitants were come together to see the
flock start on its long march. Two men and two
boys went with the gift. Goodwife Elderkin was
early on the highway. She wanted to make certain just how many sheep bore the mark of Ebenezer Devotion's ownership; but the driven sheep
went past too quickly for her, and she never had
the satisfaction of finding out how many he gave.
Following the flock up the hill, she saw in the
distance a sight that made her heart beat fast.
On the stone wall, under a great tree, sat Mary
Robbins, a little girl. She was dressed in a pink
calico frock, and she was holding in her arms a
snow-white lamb, around whose neck she had tied
a strip of the calico of which her own gown was
fashioned.

"Now if I ever saw the beat of that!" cried
Goodwife Elderkin, walking almost at a run up

the hill, and so coming to the place where the child sat, before the sheep got there.

" Mary Robbins!" she cried, breathless from her haste. " What have you got that lamb for?"

Mary blushed under her little sun-bonnet, hugged the lamb, and said not a word. At the moment up came the flock, panting and warm. Down sprang Mary Robbins from the wall, the lamb in her arms. Johnny Manning, aged fifteen years, was one of the two lads in care of the sheep. To him Mary ran, saying:

" Johnny, Johnny, won't you take my lamb, too?"

" What for?"

" Why, for some poor little girl in the town where there isn't anything to eat," urged Mary, her sun-bonnet falling unheeded into the dust, as she held up her offering to the cause of liberty.

" Why, it can't walk to Boston," said the boy, running back to recover a stray sheep.

" You can carry it in your arms," she urged.

" Give it to me, then."

She gave it, saying :

" Be good to it, Johnny, and give him some milk to drink to-night. It don't eat much grass, yet."

And so Johnny Manning marched away, over and down and out of sight, with Mary's lamb in his arms. As for Mary herself, little woman that she was, having made her sacrifice, she would have dropped on the grass, after picking up her sun-bonnet, and had a good cry over her loss, had it not been for Goodwife Elderkin standing there in the road, waiting for her.

With a sharp look at the child, the woman left
the highway to go to her own house, and Mary
went home, hoping that no one would ask her
about the lamb.

The flock of sheep marched until the noontide,
when a halt was ordered. After that they went
onward over hill and river, with rest at night and
at noon, until the town of Roxbury was reached.
At this place the sheep were left to be taken to
Boston, when opportunity could be had.

With Mary's lamb in his arms, Johnny Manning
accompanied the messenger who went up Boston
Neck to carry a letter to the " Selectmen of the
Town." That letter has been preserved and is
carefully kept among the treasured documents of
the Massachusetts Historical Society. It is too
long to be given here, but, after begging Boston
to suffer and be strong, remembering what had
been done for the country by its founders, it
closes in these words : " We know you suffer, and
feel for you. As a testimony of our commisera-
tion of your misfortunes, we have procured a
small flock of sheep, which at this season are not
so good as we could wish, but are the best we
had. This small present, gentlemen, we beg you
would accept and apply to the relief of those honest,
industrious poor, who are most oppressed by the
late oppressive acts."

Then, after a promise of future help in case of
need, the letter is signed by Samuel Grey,
Ebenezer Devotion, and seven other names, end-
ing with that of Hezekiah Manning.

" Give me the lamb, and I'll feed three hungry little girls every day as long
as Boston is shut up."

A British officer, seeing the lamb in Johnny's arms, offered to buy it, bribing him with a bit of gold; but Johnny said " there wasn't any gold in the land that he would exchange it for," and so the lamb reached Boston in safety before the sheep got there. As Johnny walked along the streets he was busy looking out for some poor little girl to give it to, according to Mary's request.

"I must wait," he thought, "until I find some one who is almost starved."

On the Common side he met a little girl who cried "Oh! see! see! A lamb! A live lamb in Boston Town!"

The child's eyes rested on the little white creature, which accosted her with a plaintive bleat. Johnny Manning's eyes were riveted on the little girl. What he thought, he never said. "Do you want it?" he asked.

"O yes! yes! Where did you get it?"

"I've brought it from Roxbury in my arms. Mary Robbins gave it, in Windham, for some poor little girl who was hungry in Boston. Are you hungry?"

"No," said the child, hesitatingly.

"Are you poor?"

"My father is"—a sudden thought stopped the words she was about to speak. "Give me the lamb," she said, "and I'll feed three hungry little girls every day as long as Boston is shut up. I will! I will! and Mary's lamb shall live until I'm a hungry little girl myself, and I will keep it until I am starved clear almost to death."

Johnny put Mary's little lamb on the walk.
"See if it will follow you," he said.

"Come lamb! lamb! come with Catharine,"
and it went bleating after her along the Common
side.

"It's used to a girl," ejaculated the boy, "and
it hasn't been a bit happy with me.   Give it grass
and milk," he called after Catharine, who turned
and bowed her head.

"A pretty story I shall have to tell Mary
Robbins," thought Johnny.   "Here I have given
her lamb to be kept and coddled, and it's likely
never eaten at all—but I know that little girl will
keep her word.   She looks it—and she said she
would feed three little girls as long as Boston is
shut up, and that is more than the lamb could do.
I must recollect the very words, to tell Mary."

When the *Boston Gazette* of July 4th, 1774,
reached the village of Windham, its inhabitants
were surprised at the following announcement,
more particularly as not one of them knew
where the *last sheep* came from:

"Last week, were driven to the neighboring town of Roxbury
two hundred and fifty-eight sheep, a generous contribution of our
sympathizing brethren of the town of Windham, in the colony of
Connecticut; to be distributed for the employment or relief of
those who may be sufferers by means of the act of Parliament,
called the Boston Port Bill."

Johnny Manning, when he returned to Windham, privately explained the matter to Mary
Robbins, by telling her that when the sheep were
numbered at Roxbury he counted in her lamb.

How One Boy Helped the British Troops out of Boston in 1776.

T was Commander-in-chief Washington's birthday, and it was Jeremy Jagger's birthday.

General Washington was forty-four years old that birthday, a hundred years ago. Jeremy Jagger was fourteen, and early in the morning of the 22d of February, 1776, the General and the lad were looking upon the same bit of country, but from different positions. General George Washington was reviewing his precious little army for the thousandth time; the lad Jeremy was looking from a hill upon the camp at Cambridge, and from thence across the River Charles over into Boston, which city had, for many months, been held by the British soldiers.

At last Jeremy exclaimed: "I say, it's too chestnut-bur bad; it is."

"Did you step on one?" questioned a tall, hard-handed, earnest-faced man, who at the instant had come up to the stone-wall on which Jeremy stood, surveying the camp and its surroundings.

"No, I didn't," retorted the lad; "but I wish Boston was *paved* all over with chestnut-burs, and that every pesky British officer in it had to walk barefoot from end to end fourteen times a day, I do; and the fourteenth time I'd order two or three Colony generals to take a turn with 'em. General Gates for one."

"Come along, Jeremy," called his companion, who had strode across the wall and gone on, regardless of the boy's words.

When Jeremy had ended his expressed wishes, he gathered up his hatchet, dinner-basket, and coil of stout cord, and plunged through the snow after his leader.

When he had overtaken him, the impulsive lad's heart burst out at the lips with the words: "*We* could take Boston *now*, just as easy as any-thing—without wasting a jot of powder either. Skip across the ice, don't you see, and be right in there before daylight. A big army lying still for months and months, and just doing nothing but wait for folks in Boston to starve out! I *say* it's shameful; now, too, when the ice has come that General Washington has been waiting all winter for."

"You won't help your country one bit by scolding about it, Jeremy. You'd better save your strength for cutting willow-rods to-day."

"I'd cut like a hurricane if the rods were only going to whip the enemy with. But just for six-pence a day—pshaw! I say, it don't pay."

"Look here, lad, can you keep a secret?"

"Trust me for that," returned Jeremy. Turning suddenly upon his questioner, he faced him to listen to a supposed bit of information.

"Then why on earth are you talking to *me* in that manner, boy?" questioned the man.

"Why you *know* all about it, just as well as I do; and a fellow *must* speak out in the woods or *somewhere*. Why, I get so mad and hot sometimes that it seems as if every thought in me would burn right out on my face, when I think about my poor mother over there," pointing backward to the three-hilled city.

The two were standing at the moment midway of a corn-field. The February wind was lifting and rustling and shaking rudely the withered corn-stalks, with their dried leaves. To the northward lay the Cambridge camp, across the Charles River. To the south and east, just over Muddy River and Stony Brook, lay the right wing of the American Army, with here a fort and there a redoubt stretching at intervals all the distance between the camp at Cambridge and Dorchester Neck, on the southeast side of Boston. Behind them, to the westward, lay Cedar Swamp, while not more than half a mile to the front there was a four-gun battery and Brookline Fort, on the Charles, near by.

While Jeremy Jagger was pouring forth his words with vociferous violence, the man by his side glanced eagerly about the wide field; but, satisfying himself that no one was within hearing, he said, resting his hatchet on the lad's shoulder while speaking: "See here, my boy. The brave man never boasts of his bravery nor the trustworthy man of his trustworthiness. How you learned what you know of the plans of General Washington I do not care to ask; but to-day and all days keep quiet and show yourself worthy of being trusted."

"I'll try as hard as I can," promised Jeremy.

"No one can have tried his best without accomplishing something that it was grand to do, though not always *just what* he was trying to do," responded the man, glancing kindly down upon the fresh, eager lad, tramping through the snow, at his side. "Don't forget. 'Silence is golden,' in war always. Not a word, mind, when you get home, about the work of to-day."

They were come now to a spot where the marsh seemed to be filled with sounds of woodcutting. As they plunged into Cedar Swamp, the sounds grew nearer and multiplied. It was like the rapid firing of muskets.

Running through the swamp there was a troutbrook, that bore along its borders a dense growth of water-willows.

And now they advanced within sight of at least two hundred men and boys, every one of whom worked away as though his life depended on cutting a certain amount of willow-boughs in a given time.

"What does it all mean?" questioned Jeremy.

"It means," replied his companion, "work for

your country to-day with all your might and main."

"But, pray tell me," persisted Jeremy, "what under the sun the things are for, anyway. They're good for nothing for fire-wood, green."

Mr. Wooster turned and looked at the lad and said: "A good soldier asks no questions and marches, without knowing whither. He also cuts, without knowing for what. Now, to work!" and, at the instant they mingled with the workmen.

In less than a minute Jeremy's dinner-basket was swinging on a willow-bough, his coat was hanging protectingly over it (you must remember that it contained Jeremy Jagger's birthday cake), and the lad's own arms were working away to the musical sounds of a hatchet beating on a vast amount of "whistle-stuff," until mid-day and hunger arrived in company.

At the signal for noon Jeremy Jagger began his birthday feast. He perched himself on a stout willow-branch, hanging the basket on a conveniently growing peg at his right hand, and, by frequent examination of the store within, was able to solace two or three lads, less fortunate than himself, who were taking the mid-day rest, refreshed by plain bread and cheese, seated on a branch, lower down on the same tree.

"It isn't *every* day that a fellow eats his birth-day dinner in the woods," he exclaimed, by way of apology for the dainties he tossed down to them in the shape of sugar-cake and "spice pie."

"Aunt Hannah was pretty liberal with me this morning. I wonder if she knew anything, for she said: ' I'd find plenty of squirrels to help eat it.' Where do you live, anyway?" he questioned, after he had fed them.

" We live in Brookline," answered the elder.

" Well, do you know what under the sun we are cutting such bundles of fagots for to-day?" he slyly questioned, being beyond the hearing of the ears of his friend, and so safe from censure.

" I asked father this morning," spoke up the younger lad (of not more than nine years), " and he told me he guessed General Washington was going to take Boston on the ice, and every soldier was going to take a bundle of fagots along, so as to keep from sinking if the ice broke through."

This bit of military news was received with shouts of laughter, that echoed from tree to tree along the brook, and then the noon-day rest was over. The wind began to blow in cooler and faster from the sea, and busy hands were obliged to work fast to keep from stiffening under the power of the growing frost.

When the new moon hung low in the west and the sun was gone, the brookside, the cart-path, even the swamp fell back into its accustomed silence, for the workers, in groups of eight or ten, had from minute to minute gone homeward, leaving hugh piles of fagots near the log bridge.

Jeremy went early to bed that night. His right arm was weary and his left arm ached;

nevertheless, he went straightway to dreaming that both arms were dragging his beloved mother forth from Boston.

At midnight his companion of the morning came and stood under his chamber window, and tapped lightly with a bean-pole against the glass to awaken him.

Jeremy heard the sound, but in his dream thought it was a gun fired from one of the ships in the harbor at his mother, and himself, and Boston.

"Jeremy, get up!" said somebody, touching his shoulder.

"Come, mother!" ejaculated Jeremy, clutching at the air and uttering the words under tremendous pressure.

"Come yourself, lad," said somebody, shaking him a little roughly; whereupon Jeremy awoke. "Get up, Jeremy Jagger. Hitch the oxen to the cart. Put on the hay-rigging. Stay, I must help you to do that; but hurry."

Jeremy rubbed his eyes, wondered what had become of his mother, and how Mr. Wooster found his way into the house in the night, and lastly, what was to be done. Furthermore, he dressed with speed, and awakened the oxen by vigorous touches and moving words.

"Get up! get up!" he importuned, "and work for your country, and may be you won't be killed and eaten for your country when you are old." The large, patient eyes of the oxen slowly

opened into the night, and after awhile the vigorous strokes and voiceful "get ups" of their
master had due effect.

Mr. Wooster helped to adjust the hay-rigging,
and then the large-wheeled cart rolled grindingly
over the frozen ground of the highway, until it
turned into the path leading into the swamp, over
which the snow lay in unbroken surface. Jeremy
Jagger's was but the pioneer cart that night. A
half-dozen rolled and tumbled and reeled over
the uneven surface behind him, to the log bridge.
It was cold and still. As the topmost fagot was
tossed on the pile in his cart he drew off a mitten,
thrust his benumbed fingers between his parted
lips, and when he removed them said: "I hope
General Washington has had a better birthday
than mine."

"I know one thing, my lad."

Jeremy turned quickly, for he did not recog-
nize the voice. Even then he could not discern
the face; but he knew instantly that it was no
common person who had spoken. Nevertheless,
with that sturdy, good-as-anybody air that made
the men of April 19th and June 17th fight so
gloriously, he demanded:

"What do you know?"

"That General Washington would gladly
change places with you to-night, if you are the
honest lad you seem to be."

"Go and see him in his comfortable bed over
there in Cambridge," was Jeremy's response,

uttered in the same breath with the word to his oxen to move on. They moved on. The fagots reeled and swayed, the cart rumbled over the logs of the bridge, and boy, oxen and cart were soon lost to sight and hearing in the cedar thickets of the swamp.

Through the next two hours they toiled on, Jeremy on foot, and often ready to lie down with the healthy sleep that would not leave its hold on his weary brain.

It was day-dawn when the fagots had been duly delivered at the appointed place and Jeremy reached home.

He had been cautiously bidden to see that the cart was not left outside with its tell-tale rigging. He obeyed the injunction, shut the oxen in, gave them double allowance of hay, and was startled by Aunt Hannah's cheery call of: "Jerry, my boy, come to breakfast."

"Breakfast ready?" said Jeremy.

"Why, yes. I was up early this morning, and thought of you." And that was the only allusion Aunt Hannah made to his night's work. He longed to tell her and chat about it all at the table; but, remembering his promise in the swamp, he said not a word.

Six nights out of seven Jeremy and his oxen worked all night and slept nearly all day.

The brook in Cedar Swamp was robbed of its willows, and many another bit of land and watercourse suffered in a like manner.

Then came the order to make the fagots into fascines. Two thousand soldiers were got to work to effect this. Jeremy Jagger began to understand what was going on behind the lines at Roxbury. He was the happiest lad in existence during the ensuing days. He forgot to eat, even, when the fascines were in making. Perceiving the manner in which they were formed he volunteered to help, and soon found he could drive the cross supports into the ground, lay the saplings upon them, and even aid in twisting the green withes about them, as well as any soldier of them all.

Bales of "screwed" hay began to appear in great numbers within the lines, and empty barrels by the hundreds sprang up from somewhere.

And all this time, guess as every man might and did—the coming event was known only to the commander-in-chief and to the six generals forming the council of war.

Monday night, before sundown, Jeremy Jagger received an order. It was:

MARCH 4TH.

JEREMY JAGGER:

With oxen and cart (hay-rigging on), be at the Roxbury lines by moon-rise to-night. Take a pocketful of gingerbread along.

WOOSTER.

With manly pride the boy set forth. He longed to put the note in his aunt's hand ere he went; but she (long ago it seemed, though only a few days had passed) seemed to take no note of his frequent absences. He had scarcely gone a rod ere the cannon-balls began their march into Boston from all the fortifications of the Americans; and in return from Boston, flying north and south and west, came shot and shells.

Undaunted and excited by the mere possibility of being hit, Jeremy went onward. When he arrived in Roxbury he found everybody and everything astir. His cart was seized, filled with bundles of "screwed" hay, and, ere he knew it, he was in line with two hundred and ninety-nine other carts, marching forward to fortify Dorchester Heights. Before him went twelve hundred troops, under the command of General Thomas; before the troops trundled an unknown number of carts, filled with intrenching tools; before the tools were eight hundred men. Not a word was spoken. In silence and with utmost care they trod the way. At eight of the clock the covering party of eight hundred reached the Height and divided—one-half going toward the point nearest Boston, the other to the point nearest Castle William, on Castle Island, held by the British.

Then the working party began their labor with enthusiasm unbounded, wondering what the British general would think when he should behold their work in the morning. They toiled in silence by the light of the moon and the home music of 144 shot and 13 shell going into Boston, and

5

unnumbered shot and shell coming out of Boston.
Gridley, whose quick night work at Breed's Hill
on the sixteenth of June had startled the world,
headed the intrenching party as engineer.

Poor Jeremy was not allowed to go farther
than Dorchester Neck with his first load. The
bundles of hay were tumbled out and laid in line,
to protect the supplying party, in case the work
going on on the hill beyond should be found out.

The next time, to his extreme delight, he found
that fascines were to go in his cart. When he
reached Dorchester Height quick work was made
of unloading his freight, and, without a word
spoken, he was ordered back with a move of the
hand.

Four times the lad and the oxen went up Dorchester Hill that night. The fourth time, as no
order was given to return, Jeremy thought he
might as well stay and see the battle that would
begin with the dawn.

He left the oxen behind an embankment with a
big bundle of hay to the front of them ; and after
five minutes devoted to gingerbread he went to
work. Morning would come long before they
were ready to have it unveil the growing forts to
the eyes of Admiral Shuldham, with his ships of
war lying in the harbor; or to the sentinels at
Castle William, on Castle Island, to the right of
them ; or to General Howe, with his vigilant
thousands of Englishmen safe and snug in Boston,
to the north of them.

Jeremy was rolling barrels to the brow of the hill they were fortifying, and tumbling into them with haste shovelful after shovelful of good solid earth, that they might hit hard when rolled down on the foe that should dare to mount the height, when a cautious voice at his side uttered the one word "Look!" accompanied with a motion of the hand toward Dorchester Neck.

In the moonlight, past the bales of hay, two thousand Americans were filing in silent haste to the relief of the men who had toiled all night to build forts they meant to defend on the morrow.

It was four o'clock in the morning when they came. Jeremy was tired and sleepy too. His eyelids would drop over his eyes, shutting out everything he so longed to keep in sight.

"You've worked like a hero," said a kind voice to the lad. "It will be hot work here by sunrise —no place for boys, when the battle begins."

"I can fight," stoutly persisted Jeremy, nodding as he spoke; and, had anybody thought of the lad at all after that, he might have been found in the ox-cart, carelessly strewn over with hay, taking a nap.

Meanwhile on came the morning. A friendly fog hung lovingly around the new hills on the old hills, that the Yankees had built in a night.

Admiral Shuldham was called in haste from his bed by frightened men, who wondered what had happened on Dorchester Height. Castle William

stood aghast with astonishment. Messengers
went up the bay to tell the army the news.

General Howe marched out to take a look
through the fog at the old familiar hills he had
known so long, and didn't like the looks of the
new hats they wore. He wondered how in the
world the thing had been done without discovery;
but there it was, larger a good deal than life, seen
through the fog, and he knew also why it was that
the cannon had been playing on Boston through
the hours of three or four nights. He was angry,
astonished, perplexed. He had a little talk with
Admiral Shuldham; and they agreed to do something. Yes, they *would* walk up and demand back
the hills looking over into Boston. Transports
came hurrying to pier and wharf, and soldiers
went bravely down and gave themselves to the
work of a short sea voyage.

Meanwhile Jeremy Jagger's nap was broken by
a number of trenching tools thrown carelessly
over his back, as he lay asleep in his cart.

"Halloo there!" he shouted, striving to rise
from the not very comfortable blanket that dropped in twain to the left and the right, as he shook
off the tools and returned from the land of sleep
to Dorchester Heights and the 5th of March.
He was just in time to hear a voice like a clarion
cry out: "Remember it is the 5th of March, and
avenge the death of your brethren."

It was the very voice that had said in the
swamp in the night that "General ·Washington

would gladly change places with Jeremy Jagger."
It was the voice of General Washington animat-
ing the troops for the coming battle.

Meanwhile a new and unexpected force arrived
on the field of action. It came in from sea—a
great and mighty wind, that tossed and tumbled
the transports to and fro on the waves and would
not let them land anywhere save at the place they
came from. So they went peacefully back to
Boston, and the Liberty Men over on the hills
went on all day and all night, in the rain and the
wind, building up, strengthening, fortifying, in
fact getting ready, as Jeremy told his aunt, when
he reached home on the morning of the sixth of
March, "for a visit from King George and all
his army."

The next day General Howe doubted and did
little. The next and the next went on and then
on the morning of the 17th of March something
new had happened. There was one little hill, so
near to Boston that it was almost in it; and lo!
in the night it had been visited by the Americans,
and a Liberty Cap perched above its head.

General Howe said : " We must get away from
here in haste."

" Take us with you," said a thousand Royalists
of the town ; and he took them, bag and baggage,
to wander up and down the earth.

Over on Bunker Breed's Hill wooden sentinels
did duty when the British soldiers left and for full
two hours after; and then two brave Yankees

guessed the men were wooden, and marched in
to take possession just nine months from the day
they bade it good-by, because they had no powder with which to " tune " their guns.

Over on Cambridge Common marched, impatient as ever, General Putnam, with his four
thousand followers, ready to cross the River
Charles and walk once more the city streets of
the good old town.   On all the hills were
gathered men, women and children to see the
British troops depart.

Jeremy Jagger was up before the dawn on that
sweetest of Sunday mornings in March, and he
reached the Roxbury lines just as General Ward
was ready to put his arms about Boston's Neck.
The lad took his place with the five hundred men
and walked by Ensign Richards' side, as he
proudly bore the standard up to the gates, which
Ebenezer Learned " unbarred and opened." Once
within the lines, Jeremy, unmindful of the crow's
feet strewn over the way, made haste through
lane and street to his old home on Beacon Hill.
" Could that be his mother looking out at him
through the window-pane ? " he thought, as he
drew near.

She saw him.   She knew him.   But what could
it mean that she did not open the door to let him
in ; that she waved him away ?   It could not be
that she, his own mother, had turned Tory, that
her face was grown so red and angry at the sight
of her son.

Jeremy banged away at the door. There was no answer.

At last he heard the lifting of a sash, a head, muffled carefully, appeared from the highest window in the house, and a voice (the lad knew whose it was) said: "Go, Jeremy! Go away out of Boston as fast as you can. I'll come to you as soon as it is safe."

"Why, mother, what's the matter?" cried the boy.

"Small pox! I've had it. Everybody has it. Go!"

"Good-by," cried Jeremy, running out of Boston as fast as any British soldier of them all and a good deal more frightened. He burst into Aunt Hannah's house with the news that he had been to Boston, that the soldiers were all gone, that he had seen his mother, that she had the small-pox and sent him off in a hurry.

"Tut! tut!" she cried. "It's wicked to tell lies, Jeremy Jagger."

"I'm not telling lies. Every word is true. Please give me something to eat."

But Aunt Hannah did not wait to give the lad food, nor even to speak the prayer of thanksgiving that went like incense from her heart. She went into the barn-yard and threw corn on the barn-floor, to which the hens and turkeys made haste. Closing the door, she summoned Jeremy to kill the largest and best of them.

That Sunday afternoon the brick oven glowed

with fervent heat, the white, fat offerings went in,
and the golden-brown turkeys and chickens came
out ; and as each, in turn, was pronounced " done,"
Aunt Hannah repeated the words: " Hungry !
hungry ! hungry ! Hungry all winter !"

The big clothes-basket was full of lint for
wounds that now never should be made. Gladly
she tossed out the fluffy mass, and packed within
it every dainty the house contained.

It was nearly sunset when Aunt Hannah and
Jeremy started forth, with the basket between
them, to Mr. Wooster's house, hoping that he
would carry it in his wagon up to Boston. He
was not at home.

" Get out the cart," said Aunt Hannah to
Jeremy, when they learned no help was to be
obtained. She sat by the roadside watching the
basket until the cart arrived.

" I'm going with you," she said, after the basket
was in ; she climbed to the seat beside the lad,
and off they started for Boston.

It was dark when they reached the lines, and
no passes granted, the officers said, to go in that
night.

" But I've food for the hungry," said Aunt
Hannah, in her sweetest voice, from the darkness
of the cart, " and folks are hungry in the night as
well as in the day."

She deftly threw aside the cover from the
basket and took out a chicken, which she held
forth to the man, saying : " Take it. It's good."

He hesitated a moment, then seized it eagerly.

" I know you," spoke up Jeremy, at this junc-
ture. " You went up the Neck with us this morning. I saw you."

" Then you are the boy who got first into
Boston this morning, are you, sir? "

" I believe I did, sir."

" Go on."

The oxen went on.

" Now, Jeremy, down with you and wait here
for me. You haven't had small-pox," said Aunt
Hannah.

" But the oxen won't mind you," said Jeremy.

Aunt Hannah was troubled. She never had
driven oxen.

At the moment who should appear but Mr.
Wooster. He gladly offered to take the basket
and deliver it at Mrs. Jagger's door.

" Don't go in, mind ! Mother's had small-pox,"
called Jeremy, as he started.

" I'm tired," gasped Aunt Hannah, who had
done baking enough for a small army that day,
as she sat down to rest on the broad seat of the
cart, and the two started for home. The soldier
at the gate scarcely heeded them as they went
out, for roasted chicken " tasted so good."

" I'm so glad the British are out of Boston,"
said Aunt Hannah, as she touched home soil
again and went wearily up the walk to the little
dark house.

" And so am I," said Jeremy to the oxen, as he

turned them in for the night; "only if I'd had
my way, they wouldn't have gone without one
good fair fight. You've done your duty, anyhow," he added, soothingly, with a parting stroke
to the honest laborer who went in last, "and you
deserve well of your country, too, for like Gen.
Washington, you have served without hope of
reward. The thing I like best about the man is
that he don't work for money. I don't want my
sixpence a day for cutting willows; and—I won't
—take it." And he didn't take it, consoling
himself with the reflection "that he would be like
Gen. Washington in one thing, anyhow."

PUSSY DEAN'S BEACON FIRE.

MARCH 17, 1776.

 HUNDRED years ago the winds of March were blowing.

To-day the same winds rush by the stone memorials and sweep across the low mounds that securely cover the men and the women that then were alive to chill blast and stirring event. Even the lads who gathered at sound of drum and fife on village green, wishing, as they saw the troopers march, that they were men, and the little girls who hung about father's neck because he was going off to war, who watched the post-riders on their course, wishing that they knew the news he carried, are no longer with us.

For nearly two years Boston had been the lost town of the people. It had been taken from the children by an unkind father and given to strangers. You have been told how British ships came and closed her harbor, so that food and raiment could not enter. You know how grandly the younger sister towns behaved toward stately, hungry Boston; how they marched up the narrow neck of land that holds back the town from

the sea, each and every one bearing gifts to the
beloved town, until there came the sad and fatal
day wherein British military lines turned back
the tide of offerings and closed the gate of
entrance.

Then it was that friends began to gather across
the rivers that wound their waters around Boston. Presently an army grew up and stationed
itself with leaders and banners and forts.

Summer came. The army waited through all
the long warm days. The summer went; the
leaves fell; the chill winds and the cold sea-fogs
wound into and out of the poor little tents and
struck the brave men who, having no tents, tried
to be strong and endure.

Every child knows, or ought to know, the story
of that winter; how day by day, all over New
England, men were striving to gather fireams and
powder wherewith to take back from the foe poor
Boston. But, alas, there was not powder enough
in all the land to do it.

The long, wearying winter had done its worst
for the prisoned inhabitants within the town; and,
truly, it had tried and pinched the waiting friends
who stood at the gates.

At last, in March, in the night, the brave
helpers climbed the hills, built on them smaller
hills, and by the light of the morning were able
to look over into the town—at which the patriots
were glad and the British commander frightened.

A little after nine of the clock on Sunday morning, the 17th of March, 1776, three Narragansett ponies stood before General Washington's head-quarters at Cambridge.

"Go with all possible speed to Governor Trumbull," said Washington, delivering despatches to a well-known and trusted messenger, who instantly mounted one of the ponies in wait-ing—Sweeping Wind by name—and rode away, with many a sharp and inquiring glance back at city and river and camp.

It was four of the clock in the afternoon, and the messenger had not paused since he set forth, longer than to give Sweeping Wind water to drink, when, on the highway in the distance, he saw a red cloak fluttering and flying before him.

It was Pussy Dean who wore the cloak. She was fifteen, fair and lovely, brave and patriotic as any soldier in the land.

At first she was angry at the law by which she was denied a new cloak that winter, made of English fabric, but when wrapped in the coveted broadcloth of scarlet belonging to her mother she was more than reconciled.

On this Sunday Pussy had been at the meeting-house on the hill, two miles from home, at both morning and afternoon service, and afterward had lingered a little to gather up bits of news from camp and town to take home to her mother, and so it had happened that she was quite alone on the highway.

Pussy chanced to look back to the summit of

the hill down which she had walked, and she saw
the express coming.

"Now," she thought, "if I could only stop
him! I wonder if I can't. I'll try, and then,"
swinging her silken bag, "I shall have news to
carry home, the very latest, too."

As she swung the bag she suddenly remembered that she had something within it to offer
the rider.

"Of course I can," she went on saying to herself. "Post-riders are always hungry, and it's
lucky for him that I didn't have to eat my dinner
myself, to-day. Now, if I only had a basketful of
clover heads or roses for that pony, I'd find out
all about Boston while it was eating."

The only roses within sight were blooming on
Pussy Dean's two cheeks as Sweeping Wind
came clattering his shoes against the frozen
ground. He would have gone straight on had a
scarlet cloak not been planted, like a fluttering
standard, full in his pathway.

The rider gave the pony the slightest possible
check, since he felt sure that no red-coated soldier
lurked behind the red cloak.

"Take something to eat, won't you?" accosted
Pussy, rather glowing in feature and agitated in
voice by her own daring.

Meanwhile the rider had given Sweeping Wind
a second intimation to stand, which he obeyed,
and sniffed at Pussy's cloak and cheeks and silken
bag as she held it forth to the rider, saying

naively, " I went to meeting and was invited to luncheon, and so didn't eat mine." She spoke swiftly, as though she knew she must not detain him.

He answered with a smile and a " Thank you," took the bag, and rewarded her by saying, " The British are getting out of Boston, bag and baggage."

"And where are you going?" demanded Pussy, determined not to go home with but half the story if she could help it.

" To Governor Trumbull with the good news and a demand for two thousand men to save New York," he cried back, having gone on. His words were entangled with a mouthful of gingerbread or mince-pie to such an extent that it was a full minute before Pussy understood their import, and then she could only say over and over to herself, as she hastened on, " Father will be here, father will come home, and we'll have the good old times back again."

But notwithstanding her hope and a country's wish, the good old times were not at hand.

Pussy reached home and told the story. Baby went down plump into the wooden cradle at the first note of it, and set up a tune of rejoicing in his own fashion which no one regarded. Brother Benjamin, aged thirteen, whistled furiously, regardless of the honors of the day. Sammy, who was ten, clapped his hands and knocked his heels together, first in joy, and then began to fear lest the war should be over before he grew big enough to be in it.

"Mother," said Pussy, a few minutes later, "let Benny come with me to tell Mr. Gale about it; may he?"

Pussy laid aside her Sunday bonnet, tied a straw hat over her ears with a silk kerchief to keep out the wind, and in three minutes got Benny into the highway.

"See here, Ben, I'm going to light a fire on Baldhead to tell all the folks together about it, and I want you to help me; quick, before it gets dark."

"You can't gather fagots," responded Ben.

Yes, she could, and would, and did, while Benny went to the house nearest to Baldhead to ask for some fire in a kettle.

The two worked with such vigor and will that the first gathering of darkness saw the light of the beacon-flame burst forth, and the great March wind blew it into fiercest glow. Every eye that saw the fire there knew that it had been kindled with a purpose, and many feet from house and hamlet set forth to learn the cause.

While Pussy and Ben were yet adding fagots to the fire, they heard a voice crying out: "The young rascals shall be punished soundly for this," and ere Pussy had time to explain or expostulate, a strong man had Ben in his grasp.

"Stop that, sir!" cried the girl, rushing to the rescue with a burning fagot that she had seized from the fire, and shaking it full in the assailant's face.

By the light of it, the man saw Pussy and she saw him ; and then both began to laugh, while Ben rubbed his ears and wondered whether they were both on his head.

"It means," spoke the girl. waving the still flaming brand toward the east, "that the British left Boston this morning, and that General"— (just here a dozen men were at the fire. Pussy raised her voice and continued)—"Washington wants you all, every one of you, to march straight to Governor Trumbull, and he'll tell you what to do next."

"If that's the case," said the responsible man of the constantly-increasing group after question-ing Pussy, "we'd better summon the militia by the ringing of the bell," and off they went in the direction of the village, while Pussy and Ben went home.

The next day saw fifty men, well armed, and provisioned for three days, on the road to Leb-anon. They marched into town and into the now famous war-office of Governor Trumbull, to his pleased surprise.

"Who sent you?" asked the governor, for it was not yet six hours since the demand on the nearest town had been made.

"Who sent us?" echoed the lieutenant, look-ing confused and at a loss to explain, and finally answering truthfully, he said : "It was a young

6

girl, your excellency. She lit a beacon fire on
a hill and gave the command that we report to
you."

A laugh ran around the sides of the old war-
office.   The messenger who had ridden from
Cambridge sat upon the counter pressing his
spurs into the wood and heard it all.

"And who commissioned the girl as a recruiting officer?" questioned the governor.

"I'm afraid," said the messenger, "I am the
guilty party. I met a young patriot in scarlet
cloak who asked my news, and, I told her."

"Where is the girl's father?" demanded
Governor Trumbull.

"He is with the army, at Cambridge," was
the response.

"And his name?"

"Reuben Dean."

A scratch or two of the quill pen was heard on
the open paper. It was folded, sealed, and
handed to the ready horseman, with the words:
"Reuben Dean; he is mentioned for promotion."

The words, as they were spoken by Governor
Trumbull, were caught up and gathered into a
mighty cheer, for every man of their number
knew that Reuben Dean was worthy of promotion, even had his daughter not gained it for him
by her services as recruiting officer.

DAVID BUSHNELL AND HIS AMERICAN TURTLE.

THE FIRST SUBMARINE BOAT INVENTED.

"DAVID!" cried a voice stern and commanding, from a house-door one morning, as the young man who owned the name was taking a short cut "across lots" in the direction of Pautapoug.

"Sir!" cried the youth in response to the call, and pausing as nearly as he could, and at the same time keep his feet from sinking into the marshy soil.

"Where are you going?" was the response.

"To Pautapoug, to see Uriah Hayden, sir."

"You'd better hire out at ship-building with him. Your college learning's of no earthly use in these days," said the father of David Bushnell, returning from the door, and sinking slowly down into his high-backed chair.

Then spoke up a sweet-voiced woman from the kitchen fire-side, where she had that moment been hanging an iron pot on the crane:

"Have a little patience, father (Mrs. Bushnell always called her husband, father), David is only looking about to see what to do. It's hardly four weeks since he was graduated."

" True enough ; but where can you find an idle man in all Saybrook town? and you know as well as I do that it makes men despise college-learning to see folks idle. I'd rather, for my part, David *did* go to work on the ship Uriah Hayden is building. 1 wish I knew what he's gone over there for to-day."

A funny smile crept into the curves of Mrs. Bushnell's lips, but her husband did not notice it.

Mr. Bushnell moved uneasily in his chair, as he sat leaning forward, both hands clasped about a hickory stick, and his chin resting on the knob at its top. Presently he said :

" Anna, I fear David is getting into bad habits. He used to talk a good deal. Now he sits with his eyes on the floor, and his forehead in wrinkles, and I'm *sure* I've heard him moving about more than one night lately, after all honest folks were in bed."

" Father, you must remember that you've been very sick, and fever gives one queer notions sometimes. I shouldn't wonder one bit if you dreamed you heard something, when 'twas only the rats behind the wainscot."

" Rats don't step like a grown man in his stocking-feet, nor make the rafters creak, either."

Madam Bushnell appeared to be investigating the contents of the pot hanging on the crane, and perhaps the heat of the blazing wood was sufficient to account for the burning of her cheeks. She cooled them a moment later by going down cellar after cider, a mug of which she offered to her husband, proposing the while that he should have his chair out of doors, and sit under the sycamore tree by the river-bank. When he assented, and she had seen him safely in the chair, she made haste to David's bed-room.

Since Mr. Bushnell's illness began, no one had ascended to the chamber except herself and her son.

On two shelves hanging against the wall were the books that he had brought home with him from Yale College, just four weeks ago.

A table was drawn near to the one window in the room. On it were bits of wood, with iron scraps, fragments of glass and copper. In fact, the same thing to-day would suggest boat-building to the mother of any lad finding them among her boy's playthings. To this mother they suggested nothing beyond the fact that David was engaged in something which he wished to keep a profound secret.

He had not told her so. It had not been necessary. She had divined it and kept silence, having all a mother's confidence in, and hope of, her son's success in life.

As she surveyed the place, she thought:

"There is nothing here, even if he (meaning her husband) should take it into his head to come up and look about."

Meanwhile young David had crossed the Pochaug River, and was half the way to Pautapoug.

All this happened more than a thousand moons ago, when all the land was aroused and astir, and David Bushnell was not in the least surprised to meet, at the ship-yard of Uriah Hayden, Jonathan Trumbull, Governor of Connecticut.

This man was everywhere, seeing to everything, in that year. Whatever his country needed, or Commander-in-chief Washington ordered from the camp at Cambridge, was forthcoming.

A ship had been demanded of Connecticut, and so Governor Trumbull had come down from Lebanon to look with his own eyes at the huge ribs of oak, thereafter to sail the seas as "The Oliver Cromwell."

The self-same oaken ribs had intense interest for young David Bushnell. Uriah Hayden had promised to sell to him all the pieces of ship-timber that should be left, and while the governor and the builder planned, he went about gathering together fragments.

" Better take enough to build a boat that will carry a seine. 'T won't cost you a mite more, and might serve you a good turn to have a sizable craft in a heavy sea some day," said Mr. Hayden.

Now David Bushnell had been wishing that he had some good and sufficient reason to give Mr. Hayden for wanting the stuff at all, and here he had given it to him.

"That's true," spoke up David, "but how am I to get all this over to Pochaug?"

"Don't get it over at all, until it's ready to row down the Connecticut, and around the Sound. You're welcome to build your boat at the yard, and, now and then, there will be odd minutes that the men can help you on with it."

David thanked Mr. Hayden, grew cheerful of heart over the prospect of owning a boat of his own, and went merrily back to the village of Pochaug.

Two weeks later David's boat was ready for sea. It was launched into the Connecticut from the ways on which the "Oliver Cromwell" grew, was named Lady Fenwick, and, when water-tight, was rowed down the river, past Saybrook and Tomb Hill, and so into the Long Island Sound.

When its owner and navigator went by Tomb Hill, he removed his hat, and bowed reverently. He thought with respect and admiration of the occupant of the sandstone tomb on its height, the Lady Fenwick who had slept there one hundred and thirty years.

With blistered palms and burning fingers David Bushnell pushed his boat with pride up the Pochaug River, and tied it to a stake at the bridge just beyond the sycamore tree, near his father's door.

"I'll fetch father and mother out to see it," he thought, "when the moon gets up a little higher."

With boyish pride he looked down at the work of his hands from the river-bank, and went in to get his supper.

"David!" called Mr. Bushnell, having heard his steps in the entry-way.

" Here I am, father," returned the young man, appearing within the room, and speaking in a cheerful tone.

"Don't you think you have wasted about time enough?"

The voice was high-wrought and nervous in the extreme. He, poor man, had been that after-noon thinking the matter over in a convalescent's weak manner of looking upon the act of another man.

David Bushnell, smiling still, and taking out a large silver watch from his waistcoat pocket, and looking at it, replied:

"I haven't wasted one moment, father. The tide was against me, but I've rowed around from Pautapoug ship-yard to the sycamore tree out here since two o'clock."

" *You* row a boat!" cried Mr. Bushnell, with lofty disdain.

"Why, father, you have not a very good opin-ion of your son, have you?" questioned the son. "Come, though, and see what he has been doing. Come, mother," as Mrs. Bushnell entered, bear-ing David's supper in her hands.

She put it down. Mr. Bushnell pulled himself upright with a groan or two, and suffered David to assist him by the support of his arm as they went out.

"Why, you tremble as though you had the palsy," said the father.

"It's nothing. I'm not used to pulling so long at the oar," said the son.

When they came to the bank, the full moon shone athwart the little boat rocking on the stream.

"What's that?" exclaimed both parents.

"That is the Lady Fenwick. I've been building the boat myself. You advised me, father, to go to ship-building one morning—do you remember? I took your advice, and began at the bottom of the ladder."

"*You* built that boat with your own hands, you say?"

"With my own·hands, sir."

"In two weeks' time?"

"Yes, sir."

"And rowed it all the way down the river, and up the Pochaug?"

"Yes, sir."

"Good boy! You may go in and have your supper," said Mr. Bushnell, patting him on the back, just as he had done when he returned from college with his first award.

As for Madam Bushnell, she smiled down upon Lady Fenwick and did her great reverence in her heart, while she said to the boat-builder:

"David, dear, wait a few minutes, and I'll give

you something nice and warm for your supper. Your father, Ezra and I had ours long ago."

That night Mr. Bushnell did not lie awake to listen for the stealthy stepping in the upper room. He slept all the sounder, because he had at last seen one stroke of honest work, as he called it, as the result of his endeavors to help David on in life.

As for David himself, he went to sleep, saying in his heart: " It is a good stepping-stone at least;" which conclusion grew into form in sleep, and shaped itself into a mighty monster, that bored itself under mountains, and, after taking a nap, roused and shook itself so mightily that the mountain flew into fragments high in air.

If you go, to-day, into the Connecticut River from Long Island Sound, you will see on its left bank the old town of Saybrook, on its right the slightly younger town of Lyme, and you will have passed by, without having been very much interested in it, an island lying just within the shelter of either bank.

In the summer of 1774 a band of fishermen put up a reel upon the island, on which to wind their seine. Over the reel they built a roof to protect it from the rains. With the exception of the reel, there was no building upon the island. A large portion of the land was submerged at the highest tides, and in the spring freshets, and was covered with a generous growth of salt grass, in which a small army might readily find concealment.

The little fishing band was now sadly broken and lessened by one of the Washingtonian demands upon Brother Jonathan. For reasons that he did not choose to give, David Bushnell joined this band of fishermen in the summer of 1775. Gradually he made himself, by purchase, the owner of the larger part of the reel and seine. In a few weeks' time he had induced his brother Ezra to become as much of a fisherman as he himself was.

As the days went by, the brothers fairly haunted this island. They gave it a name for their own use, and, early in the day-dawn of many a morning, they pulled the Lady Fenwick wearily up the Pochaug, to snatch a few winks of sleep at home, before the sun should fairly rise and call them to their daily tasks, for David assumed to help Ezra on the farm, even as Ezra helped him on the island.

The two brothers owned the reel and the seine before the end of the month of August in 1775. As soon as they became the sole owners, they procured lumber and enclosed the reel, and very seldom took down the seine from its great round perch; they used it just often enough to allay any suspicion as to their real object in becoming owners of the fishing implements.

About that time a story grew into general belief that the tomb of Lady Fenwick was haunted. Boatmen, passing in the stillness of the solemn night hours, asserted that they heard strange noises issuing from the hill, just where the lady slept in her lonely burial-place. The sounds seemed to emerge from the earth, and timid men passed up the river with every inch of sail set to catch the breeze, lest the solemn thud should sound, that a hundred persons were willing to testify had been heard by each and every one of them, at some hour of the night, coming from the tomb.

One evening in late September, the two brothers started forth as usual, nominally to "go fishing." As they stepped down the bank, Mr. Bushnell followed them.

"Boys," said he, "it's an uncommon fine night on the water. I believe I'll take a seat in your boat, with your permission. I used to like fishing myself when I was young and spry."

"And leave mother alone!" objected David.

"She's been out with me many a night on the Sound. She's brave, and won't mind a good south-west wind, such as I dare say breaks in on the shore this minute. Go and call her."

And so the family started forth to go fishing.

This was a night the two brothers had been looking forward to during weeks of earnest labor, and now—well, it could not be helped, and there was not a moment in which to hold counsel.

Mr. Bushnell had planned this surprise early in the day, but had not told his wife until evening. Then he announced his determination to "learn what all these midnight and all-night absences did mean."

As the Lady Fenwick came out from the Pochaug River into the Sound, the south-west wind brought crested waves to shore. The wind was increasing, and, to the great relief of David and Ezra, Mr. Bushnell gave the order to turn back into the river.

The next day David Bushnell asked his mother whether or not she knew the reason his father had proposed to go out with them the night before.

" Yes, David," was the reply. " I do."

" Will you tell me ? "

" He does not believe that you and Ezra go fishing at all."

" What do you believe about it, mother ? "

" I believe in *you*, David, and that when you have anything to tell to me, I shall be glad to listen."

" And father does not trust me yet ; I am sorry," said David, turning away. And then, as by a sudden impulse, he returned and said :

" If *you* can trust *me* so entirely, mother, *we* can trust *you*. To-day, two gentlemen will be here. You will please be ready to go out in the boat with us whenever they come."

" Where to ? "

" To my fishing ground, mother."

The strangers arrived, and were presented to Mrs. Bushnell as Dr. Gale and his friend, Mr. Franklin.

At three of the clock the little family set off in

the row-boat. Down at Pochaug harbor, there was Mr. Bushnell hallooing to them to be taken on board.

"I saw my family starting on an unknown voyage," he remarked, as the boat approached the shore as nearly as it could, while he waded out to meet it.

"Ah, Friend Gale, is that you?" he said, as with dripping feet he stepped in. " And whither bound?" he added, dropping into a seat.

"For the far and distant land of the unknown, Mr. Bushnell. Permit me to introduce you to my friend, Mr. Franklin."

"Franklin! Franklin!" exclaimed Mr. Bushnell, eyeing the stranger a little rudely. "*Doctor Benjamin Franklin, if you please*, Benjamin Gale!" he corrected, to the utter amazement of the party.

The oars missed the stroke, caught it again, and, for a minute, poor Dr. Franklin was confused by the sudden announcement that he existed at all, and, in particular, in that small boat on the sea.

"Yes, sir, even so," responded Dr. Gale, cheerfully adding, "and we're going down to see the new fishing tackle your son is going to catch the enemy's ships with."

"Fishing tackle! Enemy's ships! Why, David *is* the laziest man in all Saybrook town. He does nothing with his first summer but fish, fish all night long! The only stroke of honest work I've *ever* known him to do was to build this boat we're in."

During this time the brothers were pulling with a will for the island.

Arrived there, the boat was drawn up on the sand, the seine-house unlocked, and, when the light of day had been let into it, fishing-reel and seine had disappeared, and, in the language of Doctor Benjamin Gale, this is what they found therein :

THE AMERICAN TURTLE.

" The body, when standing upright, in the position in which it is navigated, has the nearest resemblance to the two upper shells of the tortoise, joined together. It is seven and a half feet long, and six feet high. The person who navigates it enters at the top. It has a brass top or cover which receives the person's head, as he sits on a seat, and is fastened on the inside by screws.

" On this brass head are fixed eight glasses, viz: two before, two on each side, one behind, and one to look out upwards. On the same brass head are fixed two brass tubes to admit fresh air when requisite, and a ventilator at the side, to free the machine from the air rendered unfit for respiration.

" On the inside is fixed a barometer, by which he can tell the depth he is under water; a compass by which he knows the course he steers. In the barometer, and on the needles of the compass, is fixed fox-fire—that is, wood that gives light in the dark. His ballast consists of about nine hundred-weight of lead, which he carries at the bottom and on the outside of the machine, part of which is so fixed as he can let run down to the bottom, and serves as an anchor by which he can ride *ad libitum*.

" He has a sounding lead fixed at the bow, by which he can take the depth of water under him, and a forcing-pump by which he can free the machine at pleasure, and can rise above water, and again immerge, as occasion requires.

" In the bow he has a pair of oars fixed like the two opposite arms of a windmill, with which he can row forward, and, turning them the opposite way, row the machine backward ; another pair, fixed upon the same model, with which he can row the machine round, either to the right or left ; and a third by which he can row the machine either up or down ; all of which are turned by foot, like a spinning wheel. The rudder by which he steers he manages by hand, within-board.

"All these shafts which pass through the machine are so curiously fixed as not to admit any water.

" The magazine for the powder is carried on the hinder part of the machine, without-board, and so contrived that, when he comes under the side of a ship, he rubs down the side until he comes to the keel, and a hook so fixed as that when it touches the keel it raises a spring which frees the magazine from the machine, and fastens it to the side of the ship ; at the same time it draws a pin, which sets the watch-work a-going, which, at a given time, springs the lock, and an explosion ensues."

Thus wrote Dr. Benjamin Gale to Silas Deane, member of Congress at Philadelphia. His letter bears the date November 9, 1775, and, after describing the wonderful machine, he adds :

" I well know the man. Lately he has conducted matters with the greatest secrecy, both for the personal safety of the navigator, and to produce the greater astonishment to those against whom it is designed ; and, you may call me a visionary, an enthusiast, or what you please, I do insist upon it that I believe the inspiration of the Almighty has given him understanding for this very purpose and design."

When the seine-house door had been fastened open, when Dr. Franklin and Dr. Gale had gone within, followed by the two brothers, Mr. Bushnell and his wife stood without looking in, and wondering in their hearts what the sight they saw could mean ; for, of the intent or purpose of the curious, oaken, iron-bound, many-paddled, brass-headed, window-lighted thing, they, it must be remembered, knew nothing. It must mean something extraordinary, of course, or Doctor Franklin would never have thought it worth his while to come out of his way to behold it.

"Father," whispered Mrs. Bushnell, "it's the *fish* David has been all summer catching."

"Fish!" ejaculated Mr. Bushnell, "it's more like a turtle."

"That's good!" spoke up Dr. Gale, from within. "Turtle it shall be."

"It is the first *submarine* boat ever made — a grand idea, wrought into substance," slowly pronounced Dr. Franklin; "let us have it forth into the river."

"And run the risk of discovery?" suggested David, pleased that his work approved itself to the man of science.

"We meant to try it last night, but failed," said Ezra Bushnell.

"There, now, father, don't you wish we had staid at home?" whispered Mrs. Bushnell.

"No!" growled the father. "They would have killed themselves getting it down alone."

He stepped within and laid his hand on the machine, saying:

"Anna, you keep watch, and, if any boat heaves in sight, let us know. Does the Turtle snap, David?" he questioned, putting forth his hand and laying it cautiously upon the animal.

7

" Never, until the word is given," replied the son, and then ten strong hands applied the strength within them to lift the curious piece of mechanism and carry it without.

The seine-house was close to the river-bank, and in a half-hour's time the American Turtle was in its native element.

Madam Anna Bushnell kept strict watch over the shores and the river, but not a sail slid into sight, not an oar troubled the waters of the tide, as it tossed back the tumble of the down-flowing river.

It was a hard duty for the mother to perform ; for, at a glance toward the bank, she saw David step into the machine, and the brass cover close down over his head. She felt suffocating fears for him, as, at last, the thing began to move into the stream. She saw it go out, she saw it slowly sinking, going down out of sight, until even the brass head was submerged.

Then she forsook her post, and hastened to the bank to keep watch with the rest.

One, two, three minutes went by. The men looked at the surface of the waters, at each other, grew thoughtful, pale ; the mother gasped and dropped on the salt grass, fainting ; the brother gave to Lady Fenwick a running push, bounded on board, and clutched the oars to row swiftly to the spot where David went down.

Mr. Bushnell filled his hat with water, and sprinkled the pale face in the sedge.

"*There! there!*" cried Dr. Franklin, with distended eyes and eager outlook.

"*Where? where?*" ejaculated Dr. Gale, striving to take into vision the whole surface of the river, at a glance.

"It's all right! He's coming up *plump!*" shouted Ezra, from his boat, as he rowed with speed for the spot where a brass tube was rising, sun-burnished, from the Connecticut.

Presently the brass head, with its very small windows, emerged, even the oaken sides were rising,—and Mr. Bushnell was greeting the returning consciousness of his wife with the words:

"It's all right, mother. David is safe."

"Don't let him know," were the first words she spoke, "that his own mother was so faithless as to doubt!"

And now, paddle, paddle, toward the river-bank came the Turtle, David Bushnell's head rising out of its shell, proud confidence shining forth from his eyes, as feet and hands busied themselves in navigating the boat that had lived for months in his brain, and now was living, in very substance, under his control.

As he neared the bank a shout of acclamation greeted him.

He reached the island, was fairly dragged forth from his seat, and carried up to the spot where his mother sat, trying to overcome every trace of past doubt and fear.

"Now," said Dr. Gale, "let us give thanks unto

Him who hath given this youth understanding to do this great work."

With bared heads and devout hearts the thanksgiving went upward, and thereafter a perfect shower of questions pelted David Bushnell concerning his device to blow up ships : *how* he came to think of it at all—*where* he got this idea and that as to its construction—to all of which he simply said :

"*You'll find your answer in the prayer you've just offered !* "

" But," said practical Mr. Bushnell, "the Lord did not send you money to buy oak and iron and brass, did he?"

"Yes," returned David, "by the hand of my good friend, Dr. Gale. To him belongs half the victory."

" Pshaw! pshaw!" impatiently uttered the doctor. "I tell you it is *no such thing!* I only advanced My Lady here," turning to Madam Bushnell, "a little money, on her promise to pay me at some future time. I'm mightily ashamed *now* that I took the promise at all. Madam Bushnell, I'll never take a penny of it back again, *never*, as long as I live. I *will* have a little of the credit of this achievement, and no one shall hinder me."

" How is that, mother?" questioned Mr. Bushnell. "*You* borrow money and not tell me!" and David and Ezra looked at her.

" I—I— " stammered forth the woman, " I only *guessed* that David was doing something that he wanted money for, and told Dr. Gale if he gave it to him I would repay it. Do you *care*, father?"

Before he had a chance to get an answer in, David Bushnell stepped forward, and, taking the little figure of his mother in his arms, kissed her sharply, and walked away, to give some imaginary attention to the Turtle at the bank.

"It is a fair land to work for!" spoke up Doctor Franklin, looking about upon river and earth and sea; "worthy it is of our highest efforts; of our lives, even, if need be. God give us strength as our need *shall* be."

With many a tug and pull and hearty heave-ho, the Turtle was hoisted up the bank and safely drawn into the seine-house. The door was locked, and Lady Fenwick's tomb gave forth no sound that night.

Doctor Franklin went his way to Boston. Doctor Gale returned to Killingworth and his waiting patients, and the Bushnells, father, mother and sons, having put the two gentlemen on the Saybrook shore, went down the river into the Sound, along its edge, and up the small Pochaug to their own home by the sycamore tree.

Mr. Bushnell and Ezra did the rowing that night. David's white hands had, somehow, a new radiance in them for his father's eyes, and did not seem exactly fitted for rowing just a common boat and every-day oars.

The young man sat in the stern, beside his mother, one arm around her waist, and the other clasped closely between her little palms, while, now and then, her finding eyes would penetrate his consciousness with a glance that seemed to say, " I always believed in you, David."

If you go to-day and stand upon the site of the old fort, built at the mouth of the Connecticut River, in the year 1635, by Lion Gardiner, once engineer in the service of the Prince of Orange, and search the waters up and down for the island on which David Bushnell built the American Turtle in 1775, you will not find it.

If you seek the oldest inhabitant of Saybrook, and ask him to point out its locality, he will say, with boyhood's fondness for olden play-grounds in his tone:

"Ah, yes! It is *Poverty* Island that you mean. It used to be there, but spring freshets and beating storms have washed it away."

The unexpected visit of Dr. Benjamin Franklin, to see the machine David Bushnell was building, gave new force to that young gentleman's confidence in his own powers of invention.

He worked with increased energy and hope to perfect boat and magazine, that he might do good service with them before winter should fall on the waters of the Massachusetts Bay, where the hostile ships were lying.

At last came the day wherein the final trial-trip should be made. The pumps built by Mr. Doolittle, but not according to order, had failed once, but new ones had been supplied, and everything seemed propitious. David and Ezra, with their mother in the boat, rowed once more to Poverty Island. "On the morrow the great venture should begin," they said.

The time was mid-October. The forests had wrapped the cooling coast in warmth of coloring that was soft and many-hued as the shawls of Cashmere, while the sun-made fringe of goldenrod fell along the shores of river and island and sea.

Mrs. Bushnell's heart beat proudly above the fond affection that could not suppress a shiver, as the Turtle was pushed into the stream. She could not help seeing that David made a line fast from the seine-house to his boat ere he went down. They watched many minutes to see him rise to the surface, but he did not.

"Mother," said Ezra, "the pump for forcing water out when he wants to rise don't work, and we must pull him in. He feared it."

As he spoke the words he laid hold on the line, and began gently to draw on it.

"Hurry! hurry! *do!*" cried Mrs. Bushnell, seizing the same line close to the water's edge, and drawing on it with all her strength. She was vexed that Ezra had not told her the danger in the beginning, and she "knew *very* well that

SHE would not have stood there and let David die of suffocation, in that horrid, brass-topped coffin!"

"Hold, mother!" cried Ezra; "pull gently, or the line may part on some barnacled rock if it gets caught."

Nevertheless, Mrs. Bushnell pulled in as fast as she could.

The tide was sweeping up the river, and a shark, in hard chase after a school of menhaden, swam steadily up, with fin out of water.

Just as the shark reached the place, he made a dive, and the rope parted!

Mrs. Bushnell screamed a word or two of the terror that had seized her. Ezra looked up, amazed to find the rope coming in so readily, hand over hand. He cast it down, sprang to the boat, and pushed off to the possible rescue, only to find that the Turtle was making for the river-bank instead of the island.

He rowed to the spot. His brother, for the first time in his life, was overcome with disappointment and disinclined to talk.

"I — I," said David, wiping his forehead. "I grew tired, and made for shore. The tide was taking me up fast."

"Did you let go the line?" questioned Ezra.

"Yes."

"The pump works all right, then?"

"Yes."

"You've frightened mother terribly."

" Have I ? I never thought. I *forgot* she was
here.   Let us get back, then;" and the two
brothers, without speaking a word, rowed down
against the sweep of tide, the great Turtle in tow.

The three went home, still keeping a silence
broken only by briefest possible question and
answer.

The golden October night fell upon the old
town.   Pochaug River, its lone line of silver
gathered in many a stretch of interval into which
the moon looked calmly down, lay on the land
for many a mile.

Again and again, during the evening, David
Bushnell went out from the house and stood
silently on the rough bridge that crossed the
river by the door.

" Let David alone, mother," urged Ezra, as she
was about to follow him on one occasion.   " He
is thinking out something, and is better alone."

That which the young man was thinking at the
moment was, that he wished the moon would
hurry and go down.   He longed for darkness.

The night was growing cold. Frost was in the air.

As he stood on the rough logs, a post-rider,
hurrying by with letters, came up.

" Holloa there !" he called aloud, not liking the
looks of the man on the bridge.

" It's I,—David Bushnell, Joe Downs ! You can
ride by in safety," he responded, ringing out one
of his merriest chimes of laughter at the very
idea of being taken for a highwayman.

"I've news," said Joe ; "want it?"

"Yes."

Joe Downs opened his pocket, and, by the light of the moon, found the letter he had referred to.

"Dr. Gale told me not to fail to put this into your hands as I came by. I should kind o' judge, by the way he *spoke*, that the continent couldn't get along very well *'thout you*, if I hadn't known a thing or two. Howsomever, here's the letter, and I've to jog on to Guilford afore the moon goes down. So good-night."

"Good night, Joe. Thank you for stopping," said David, going into the house.

"Were you expecting that letter, David?" questioned Mr. Bushnell, when it had been read.

"No, sir. It is from Dr. Gale. He asks me to hasten matters as far as possible, but a new contrivance will have to go in before I am ready."

"There! *That's* what troubles him," thought both Mrs. Bushnell and Ezra, and they exchanged glances of sympathy and satisfaction—and the little household went to sleep, quite care-free that night.

At two of the clock, with nearly noiseless tread, David Bushnell left the house.

As the door closed his mother moved uneasily in her sleep, and awoke with the sudden consciousness that something uncanny had happened. She looked from a window and saw, by the light of a low-lying moon, that David had gone out.

Without awakening her husband she protected herself with needful clothing, and, wrapped about in one of the curious plaid blankets of mingled blue and white, adorned with white fringe, that are yet to be found in the land, she followed into the night.

Save for the sleepy tinkle of the water over the stones in the Pochaug River, and an occasional cry of a night-bird still lingering by the sea, the air was very still.

With light tread across the bridge she ran a little way, and then ventured a timid cry of her own into the night :

" David ! David !"

Now David Bushnell hoped to escape without awakening his mother. He was lingering near, to learn whether his going had disturbed anyone, and he was quite prepared for the call.

Turning back to meet her he thought : " *What* a mother *mine* is." And he said, " Well, mother, what is it ? I was afraid I might disturb you."

" O David !" was all that she could utter in response.

" And so *you* are troubled about me, are you ? I'm only going to chase the will-o'-the.wisp a little while, and I could not do it, you know, until moon-down."

" *O* David !" and this time with emphatic pres-sure on his arm, " David, come home. *I* can't let you go off alone."

" Come with me, then. You're well blanketed,

I see. I'd much rather have some one with me, only Ezra was tired and sleepy."

He said this with so much of his accustomed manner that Mrs. Bushnell put her hand within his arm and went on, quite content now, and willing that he should speak when it pleased him to do so, and it pleased him very soon.

" Little mother," he said, " I am afraid you are losing faith in me."

" Never! David; only—I *was* a little afraid that you were losing your own head, or faith in yourself."

" No; but I *am* afraid I've lost my faith in something else. I showed you the two bits of fox-fire that were crossed on one end of the needle in the compass, and the one bit made fast to the other? Well, to-day, when I went to the bottom of the river, the fox-fire gave no light, and the compass was useless. Can you understand how bad that would be under an enemy's ship, not to know in which direction to navigate?"

" You must have fresh fire, then."

" *That* is just what I am out for to-night. I had to wait till the moon was gone."

" Oh! is *that* all? How foolish I have been! but you ought to tell me some things, sometimes, David."

" And so I will. I tell you now that it will be well for you to go home and go to sleep. I may have to go deep into the woods to find the fire I want."

But his mother only walked by his side a little faster than before, and on they went to a place where a bit of woodland had grown up above fallen trees.

They searched in places wherein both had seen the fire of decaying wood a hundred times, but not one gleam of phosphorescence could be found anywhere. At last they turned to go homeward.

" What will you do, David? Go and search in the Killingworth woods to-morrow night?" she asked, as they drew near home.

" It is of no use," he said, with a sigh. " It *must* be that the frost destroys the fox-fire. Unless Dr. Franklin knows of a light that will not eat up the air, everything must be put off until spring."

The next day David Bushnell went to Killingworth, to tell the story to Dr. Gale, and Dr. Gale wrote to Silas Deane (Conn. Historical Col., Vol. 2), begging him to inquire of Dr. Franklin concerning the possibility of using the Philosopher's Lantern, but no light was found, and the poor Turtle was housed in the seine-house on Poverty Island during the long winter, which proved to be one of great mildness from late December to mid-February.

In February we find David Bushnell before Governor Jonathan Trumbull and his Council at Lebanon, to tell about and illustrate the marvels of his wonderful machine.

During this time the whole affair had been kept

a profound secret from all but the faithful few surrounding the inventor. And now, if ever, the time was drawing near wherein the labor and outlay must either repay laborer and lender, or give to both great trouble and distress.

I cannot tell you with what trepidation the young man walked into the War Office at Lebanon, with a very small Turtle under his arm.

You will please remember the situation of the colonists at that moment. On the land they feared not to contend with Englishmen. Love of liberty in the Provincials was strong enough, when united with a trusty musket and a fair supply of powder, to encounter red-coated regulars of the British army; but on the ocean, and in every bay, harbor and river, they were powerless. The enemy's ships had kept Boston in siege for nearly two years, the Americans having no opposing force to contend with them.

Could this little Turtle, which David Bushnell carried under his arm, do the work he wished it to, why, every ship of the line could be blown into the air!

The inventor had faith in his invention, but he feared, when he looked into the faces of the grave Governor and his Council of War, that he could *never* impart his own belief to them.

I cannot tell you with what trust of heart and faith of soul Mrs. Bushnell kept the February day in the house by the bridge at Pochaug. Even the strong-minded, sturdy-nerved Mr. Bush-

nell looked often up the road by which David
and Ezra would approach from Lebanon, with a
keen interest in his eyes; but he would not let
any word escape him, until darkness had fallen
and they were not come.

"He said he would be here at eight, at the
very latest," said the mother at length, and she
went to the fire and placed before the burning
coals two chickens to broil.

"I'm afraid David won't have much appetite,
unless his model *should* be approved, and money
is too precious to spend on *experiments*," said Mr.
Bushnell, as she returned to his side.

"Do you mean to tell me you *doubt?*"

"Of course I doubt. Jonathan Trumbull is a
man not at all likely to give his consent to anything
that does not commend itself to common sense."

Mr. Bushnell was saved the pain of saying his
thought, that he was afraid, if David's plan was a
good one, *somebody* would have thought of it long
ago, for vigorous knuckles were at work upon
the winter-door.

As soon as it was opened the genial form of
good Dr. Gale stood revealed.

"Are the boys back yet?" he asked, stepping
within.

"No, but we expect them every minute," said
Mr. Bushnell.

"Well, friends, I had a patient within three
miles of you to visit, and I thought I'd come on
and hear the news."

Ere he was fully made welcome to hearth and home, in walked David, with the little Turtle under his arm. Without ado he went up to his mother and said :

" Madam, I present this to you, with Governor Trumbull's compliments. He has ordered your boy money, men, metals and powder without stint to work with. *Wish me joy, won't you ?* "

I do not anywhere find a record of the words in which the joy was wished, on that 2nd of February, a hundred years ago, but it is easy to imagine the very tones in which the good, God-loving Dr. Gale gave thanks for the new blessing that had that day fallen on his friend's house.

It is impossible to follow David Bushnell in his many journeys to the iron furnaces of Salisbury, in the spring and early summer of 1776, during which time the entire country was aroused and astir from the removal of the American army from Boston to New York; and our friends at Saybrook were busy as bees from morning till night, in getting ready perfect machines for duty,

David Bushnell's strength proved insufficient to navigate one of his Turtles in the tidal waters of the Sound, and his brother Ezra learned to do it most perfectly.

In the latter end of June, the British fleet, which had sailed out of Boston harbor so ingloriously on the 17th of March, for Halifax, there to await re-inforcements, appeared in waters adjacent to New York.

The signal of their approach was gladly hailed by the inventor and by the navigator of the American Turtle.

A whale-boat from New London, her seamen sworn to inviolable secrecy, was ordered to be in the river at a given point, on a given night, for a service of which the men were utterly ignorant.

On the evening previous, Ezra Bushnell, over-worn by many attempts at navigating the machine, was taken seriously ill. At midnight he was delirious—at day-dawn Dr. Gale was sent for.

When night fell he was in a raging fever, with no prospect of rapid recovery.

David set off alone, and with a heavy heart, to meet the boatmen. In the seine-house on Poverty Island the brothers had stored provisions for a cruise of several days. To this spot David Bush-nell went alone, and with a saddened heart, for he knew that it must be many days ere he could learn of his brother's condition.

The New London boatmen were promptly at the appointed place of meeting.

When they saw the curious thing they were told to take in tow, their curiosity knew no bounds; and it was only when assured that it was dangerous to examine it, that they desisted from their determination to know all about it, and con-sented to obey orders.

When, at last, a departure was made, the hour was midnight, the tide served, and no ill-timed discovery was made of the deed.

8

The strong-armed boatmen rowed well and long, and, as daylight dawned, they were directed to keep a look-out for Faulkner's Island, a small bit of land in the Sound, nearly five miles from the Connecticut shore.

The flashing light that illumines the waters at night for us, did not gleam on them, but nevertheless, the high brown bank and the little slope of land looked inviting to weary men, as they cautiously rowed near to it, not knowing whom they might meet there.

They landed, made a fire, cooked their food, ate of it, and lay down to sleep until night should come again.

They set out early in the ensuing twilight, and rowed westward all night, in the face of a gentle wind.

"If there were only another Faulkner's Island to flee to," said Mr. Bushnell, as morning drew near. "Do you know (to one of the men) a safe place to hide in on this coast?"

They were then off Merwin's Point, and between West Haven and Milford.

"There's Poquahaug," was the reply, with a momentary catch of the oar, and incline of the head toward the south-west.

"*What* is Poquahaug?"

"A little island, pretty well in, close to shore, as it were, and, maybe, deserted."

After deliberate council had been held it was resolved to examine the locality.

A few years after New Haven and Milford churches were formed under the oak-tree at New Haven, this little island, to which they were fleeing to hide the Turtle from daylight, was "granted to Charles Deal for a tobacco plantation, provided that he would not trade with the Dutch or Indians;" but now Indians, Dutch and Charles Deal alike had left it, the latter with a rude, sheltering building in place of Ansantawae's big summer wigwam that used to adorn its crest.

To this spot, bright with grass, and green with full-foliaged trees of oak on its eastern shore, the weary boatmen, who had had a long, hard pull of twenty miles to make, came, just as the longest day's sun was at its rising.

They were so glad and relieved *and* satisfied to find no one on it.

The Turtle was left at anchor near the shore; the whale-boat gave up of its provisions, and presently the little camp was in the enjoyment of a long day of rest and refreshment.

Should anyone approach from the seaward or from the mainland, it was determined that the party should resolve itself into a band of fishermen, fishing for striped bass, for which the locality was well known.

As the day wore on, and the falling tide revealed a line of stones that gradually increased, as the water fell, to a bar a hundred feet wide, stretching from the island to the sands of the Connecticut shore, David Bushnell perceived that the locality was just the proper place in which to learn and teach the art of navigating the Turtle. He examined the region well, and then called the men together.

They were staunch, good-hearted fellows, accustomed to long pulls in northern seas after whales, and that they were patriotic he fully believed. The Turtle was drawn up under the grassy bank, where the long sedge half hid, and bushels of rock-weed and sea-drift wholly concealed it, and then, in a few carefully-chosen words, David Bushnell entrusted it to the watch and care of the boatmen.

"I am going to leave it here, and you with it, until I return," he said. "Guard it with your lives if need be. If you handle it, it will be at the risk of life. If you keep it *well*, Congress will reward you.

The mystery of the whole affair enchanted the men. They made faithful promises, and, in the glorious twilight of the evening, rowed David Bushnell across the beautiful stretch of Sound that to-day separates Charles Island from the comely old town of Milford.

As the whale-boat went up the harbor, a sailing vessel was getting ready to depart.

Finding that it was bound to New York, David Bushnell took passage in it the same night.

Two days later, with a letter from Governor Trumbull to General Washington as his introduction, the young man, by command of the latter, sought out General Parsons, and "requested him to furnish him with two or three men to learn the navigation of his new machine. General Parsons immediately sent for Ezra Lee, then a sergeant, and two others, who had *offered* their services to go on board a fireship; and, on Bushnell's request being made known to them, they enlisted themselves under him for this novel piece of service."

Returning to Poquahaug (the Indian name of Charles Island), the American Turtle was found safe and sound. Here the little party spent many days in experimenting with it in the waters about the island; and in the Housatonic River.

During this time the enemy had got possession of a portion of Long Island, and of Governor's Island in the harbor—thus preventing the approach to New York by the East River.

When the appalling news of the battle of Long Island reached David Bushnell, he resolved, cost what it might of danger to himself, or hazard to the Turtle, to get it to New York with all speed.

To that end he had it conveyed by water to New Rochelle, there landed and carried across the country to the Hudson River, and presently we hear of it as being on a certain night, late in August, ready to start on its perilous enterprise.

If you will go to-day and stand where the Turtle floated that night (for the land has since that time grown outward into the sea), on your right hand across the Hudson River, you will see New

Jersey. At your left, across the East River, Long Island begins, with the beautiful Governor's Island in the bay just before you, and, looking to the southward, in the distance, you will discern Staten Island.

Let us go back to that day and hour.

The precise date of the Turtle's voyage down the bay is not given, but the time must have been on the night of either the thirtieth or thirty-first of August. We will choose the thirtieth, and imagine ourselves standing in the crowd by the side of Generals Washington and Putnam, to see the machine start.

Remember, now, where we stand. It is only *last* night that *our* army, defeated, dispirited, exhausted by battle, lay across the river on Brooklyn Heights. Behind it, busy with pickaxe and shovel, the victorious troops of Mother England were making ready to "finish" the Americans on the morrow.

There were supposed to be twenty-four thousand of the enemy, only nine thousand Continentals; and, just ready to enter East River and cut them off from New York, lay the British fleet to the north of Staten Island.

As happened at Boston in March, so happened it last night in New York, a friendly fog held the heights of Brooklyn in its grasp, while at New York all was clear.

Under cover of this fog General Washington withdrew across the river, a mile or more in width, *nine thousand men*, with all their "baggage, stores, provisions, horses, and munitions of war," and not a man of the enemy knew that they were gone until the fog lifted.

Now, as we stand, Long Island, Governor's Island, Staten Island, one and all are under the control of Britons.

David Bushnell is in a whale-boat, down close to the Turtle, giving some last important words of direction to brave Ezra Lee, who has stepped within it. David Bushnell could not help wishing, as he did so, that he could take his place and guide the spirit of the child of his own creation, in its first great encounter with the world.

The word is given. The brass top of the Turtle is shut down. Watchful eyes and swift rowers belonging to the enemy are keeping guard on Governor's Island, by which Ezra Lee must row, and it is safer to go under water. How crowded this little pier would be, did the inhabitants but know what is going on!

The whale-boats start out, David Bushnell in one of them. They mean to take the Turtle in tow the minute it is safe to do so and save Ezra Lee the labor of rowing it until the last minute.

It is eleven o'clock. All silently they dip the oars, and hear the sentinels cry from camp and shore.

Past the island, in safety, at last. They look for the Turtle. Up it comes, a distant watch-light gleaming across its brass head disclosing its presence.   Once more it is in tow, and Lee is in the whale-boat.

Down the bay they go, until the lights from the fleet grow dangerously near.

On the wide, wind-stirred waters of New York Bay, Ezra Lee gets into the Turtle, and is cast off, and left alone, for the whale-boats return to New York.

With the rudder in his hand, and his *feet* upon the oars, he pursues his way.   The strong ebb tide flows fast, and, before he is aware of it, it has drifted him down past the men-of-war.

However, he immediately *gets the machine about*, and, " by hard labor at the crank for the space of five glasses by the ships' bells, or two and a half hours, he arrives under the stern of one of the ships at about slack water."

Day is now beginning to dawn.   He can see the people on board, and hear them talk.

The moment has come for diving.   He closes up quickly overhead, lets in the water, and goes down under the ship's bottom.

He now applies the screw and does all in his power to make it enter, but in vain ; it will not pierce the ship's copper.   Undaunted, he paddles along to a different part, hoping to find a softer place ; but, in doing this, in his hurry and excitement, he manages the mechanism so that the Turtle instantly arises to the surface on the east side of the ship, and is at once exposed to the piercing light of day.

Again he goes under, hoping that he has not been seen.

This time his courage fails. It is getting to be day. If the ship's boats are sent after him his escape will be very difficult, well-nigh impossible, and, if he saves himself at all, it must be by rowing more than four miles.

He gives up the enterprise with reluctance, and starts for New York.

Governor's Island *must* be passed by. He draws near to it, as near as he can venture, and then submerges the Turtle. Alas! something has befallen the compass. It will not guide the rowing under the sea.

Every few minutes he is compelled to rise to the surface to look out from the top of the machine to guide his course, and his track grows very ziz-zag through the waters.

Ah! the soldiers at Governor's Island see the Turtle! Hundreds are gathering upon the parapet to watch its motions, such a curious boat as it is, with turret of brass bobbing up and down, sinking, disappearing—coming to the surface again in a manner *wholly* unaccountable.

Brave Lee knows his danger, and paddles away for dear life and love of family up in Lyme, eating breakfast quietly now he remembers, not knowing his peril.

Once more he goes up to take a lookout, to see where White-hall slip lies.

A glance at Governor's Island, and he sees a barge shove off laden with his enemies.

Down again, and up, and he sees it making for him. *There is no escape!* What *can* he do!

"If I must die," he thinks, "they shall die with me!" and he lets go the magazine.

Nearer and nearer—the barge is *very* close. "If they pick me up they will pick that up," thinks Lee, "and we shall all be blown to atoms together!"

They are now within a hundred and fifty feet of the Turtle and they see the magazine that he has detached.

"Some horrible Yankee trick!" cries a British soldier. "*Beware!*" And they do beware by turning and rowing with all speed for the island whence they came.

Poor Lee looks out with amazement to see them go. He is well-nigh exhausted, *and the magazine, with its dreadful clock-work going on within it, and its hundred and fifty pounds of powder, ready to go off at a given moment*, is floating on behind him, borne by the tide.

He strains every muscle to near New York. He signals the shore.

Since daylight Putnam has been there keeping watch. David Bushnell has paced up and down all night, in keen anxiety.

The friendly whale-boats put out to meet him.

Meanwhile, slowly borne by the coming tide, the magazine floats into the East River.

" It will blow up in five minutes now," says Bushnell, looking at his watch, and he goes to welcome Ezra Lee.

The five minutes go by.

Suddenly, with tremendous voice, and awful uproar of the sea, the magazine explodes.

Columns of water toss high in air, mingled with the oaken ribs that held the powder but a minute ago.

Consternation seizes British troops on Long Island. The brave soldiers on the parapet at Governor's Island quake with fear. All New York rushes to the river-side to find out what it can mean. Nothing, on all the face of the earth, *ever* happened like it before, one and all declare.

Opinion varies concerning it, from bomb to earthquake, from meteor to water-spout, and settles down on neither.

Poor Ezra Lee feels that he *meant* well, but did not act wisely. David Bushnell praises the sergeant, and takes all the want of success to himself, in not going to do his own work.

Meanwhile, with astonishment, Generals Washington and Putnam and David Bushnell himself behold, as did the Provincials, *after* the battle of *Bunker-Breed's* Hill, *victory in defeat*, for lo! no British ship sails up the East River, or appears to bombard New York.

Silently they weigh anchor and drop down the bay. The little American Turtle gained a bloodless victory that day.

Note.—The writer has carefully followed, in the account of the Turtle's attempt upon the Eagle, the statement of **Ezra Lee**, made to Mr. Charles Griswold of Lyme, more than forty years after the occurrence, and by him communicated to the *American Journal of Science and Arts* in 1820. For the description of the wonderful mechanism of the machine, the account given *at the time* by Dr. Gale in his letters to Silas Deane has been chosen, as probably more accurate than one made from memory after forty years had passed.

David Bushnell was appointed from civil life Captain-Lieutenant of a Corps of Sappers and Miners—recommended for the position by Governor Trumbull, General Parsons and others. June 8, 1781, he was promoted full Captain. He was present at the siege of Yorktown and commanded the Corps in 1783.

He was also a member of the Society of the Cincinnati.

THE BIRTHDAY OF OUR NATION.

ELLMAN GREY and Blue-Eyed Boy were hurrying up Chestnut street; the man carried a large key, the boy a new broom.

It was a very warm morning in a very warm month of a very warm year; in fact it may as well be stated at once that it was the Fourth day of July, 1776, and that Bellman Grey and Blue-Eyed Boy were in haste to make ready the State House of Pennsylvania for the birth of the United States of America. No wonder they were in a hurry.

In fact, everybody seemed in a hurry that day; for before Bellman Grey had whisked that new broom over the floor of Congress Hall, in walked, arm-in-arm, Thomas Jefferson and John Adams.

"Good morning, gentlemen," said Bellman Grey. "You'll find the dust settled in the committee-room. I'm cleaning house a little extra to-day for the expected visitor.".

"For the coming heir?" said Mr. Adams.

"When Liberty comes, She comes to stay," said Mr. Jefferson, half-suffocated with the dust; and the two retreated to the committee-room.

Blue-Eyed Boy was polishing with his silken duster the red morocco of a chair as the gentle-

men opened the door. He heard one of them
say, " If Cæsar Rodney gets here, it will be
done."

" If it's done," said the boy, " won't you, please,
Mr. Adams, won't you, please, Mr. Jefferson, let
me carry the news to General Washington?"

The two gentlemen looked either at the other,
and both at the lad, in smiling wonder.

" If what is done?" asked Mr. Adams.

" If the thing is voted and signed and made
sure," (just here Blue-Eyed Boy waved his duster of a flag and stood himself as erect as a flag-
pole ;) " if the tree's transplanted, if the ship gets
off the ways, if we run clear away from King
George, sir; so far away that he'll never catch
us."

" And why do you, my lad, wish to carry the
news to General Washington?" asked Mr. Jefferson.

" Because," said the boy, " why—wouldn't you?·
It'll be jolly work for the soldiers when they
know they can fight for themselves."

Just here Bellman Grey shouted for Blue-Eyed
Boy, bidding him come quick and be spry with
his dusting, too.

Before the hall was cleared of the accumulated
dust of State-rooms above and Congress-rooms
below, in came members of the Congress, one-by-
one and two-by-two, and in groups. The doors
were locked, and the solemn deliberations began.
Within that room, now known as Independence

Hall, sat, in solemn conclave, half a hundred men, each and every one of whom knew full well that the deed about to be done would endanger his own life.

On a table lay a paper, awaiting signatures. A silver ink-stand held the ink that trembled and wavered to the sound and stir of John Adams's voice, as he stated once more the why and the wherefore of the step America was about to take.

This final statement was made for the especial enlightenment of three gentlemen, new members of the Congress from New Jersey, and in reply to the reasons given by Mr. Dickinson why the Declaration of Independence should *not* be made.

In the meantime Bellman Grey was up in the steeple, "seeing what he could see," and Blue-Eyed Boy was answering knocks at the entrance doors; then running up the stairs to tell the scraps of news that he had gleaned through open door, or crack, or key-hole.

The day wore on; outside a great and greater crowd surged every moment against the walls; but the walls of the State House were thick, and the crowd was hushed to silence, with intense longing to hear what was going on inside.

From his high-up place in the belfry, where he had been on watch, Bellman Grey espied a figure on horseback, hurrying toward the scene; the horse was white with heat and hurry; the rider's "face was no bigger than an apple," but it was a face of importance that day.

"Run!" shouted Bellman Grey from the belfry. "Run and tell them that Mr. Rodney comes."

The boy descended the staircase with a bound and a leap and a thump against the door, and announced Cæsar Rodney's approach.

In he came, weary with his eighty miles in the saddle, through heat and hunger and dust, for Delaware had sent her son in haste to the scene.

The door closed behind him and all was as still and solemn as before.

Up in the belfry the old man stroked fondly the tongue of the bell, and softly said under his breath again and again as the hours went: "They will never do it; they will never do it."

The boy sat on the lowest step of the staircase, alternately peeping through the key-hole with eye to see and with ear to hear. At last, came a stir within the room. He peeped again. He saw Mr. Hancock, with white and solemn face, bend over the paper on the table, stretch forth his hand, and dip the pen in the ink. He watched that hand and arm curve the pen to and fro over the paper, and then he was away up the stairs like a cat.

Breathless with haste, he cried up the belfry: "*He's a doing it, he is!* I saw him through the key-hole. Mr. Hancock has put his name to that big paper on the table."

"Go back! go back! you young fool, and keep watch, and tell me quick when to ring!" cried down the voice of Bellman Grey, as he wiped for the hundredth time the damp heat from his forehead and the dust from the iron tongue beside him.

Blue-Eyed Boy went back and peeped again just in time to see Mr. Samuel Adams in the chair, pen in hand.

One by one, in "solemn silence all," the members wrote their names, each one knowing full well, that unless the Colonists could fight longer and stronger than Great Britain, that signature would prove his own death-warrant.

It was fitting that the men who wrote their names that day should write with solemn deliberation.

Blue-Eyed Boy peeped again. "I hope they're almost done," he sighed; "and I reckon they are, for Mr. Rodney has the pen now. My! how tired and hot his face looks! I don't believe he has had any more dinner to-day than I have, and I feel most awful empty. It's almost night by this time, too."

At length the long list was complete. Every man then present had signed the Declaration of Independence, except Mr. Dickinson of Pennsylvania.

And now came the moment wherein the news should begin its journey around the world. The Speaker, Mr. Thompson, arose and made the announcement to the very men who already knew it.

9

Blue-Eyed Boy peeped with his ear and heard the words through the key-hole.

With a shout and a cry of "Ring! ring!" and a clapping of hands, he rushed upward to the belfry. The words, springing from his lips like arrows, sped their way into the ears and hands of Bellman Grey. Grasping the iron tongue of the old bell, backward and forward he hurled it a hundred times, its loud voice proclaiming to all the people that down in Independence Hall a new nation was born to the earth that day.

When the members heard its tones swinging out the joyous notes they marvelled, because no one had authorized the announcement. When the key was turned from within, and the door opened, there stood the mystery facing them, in the person of Blue-Eyed Boy.

"I told him to ring; I heard the news!" he shouted, and opened the State House doors to let the Congress out and all the world in.

You know the rest; the acclamation of the multitude, the common peals (they forgot to be careful of powder that night in the staid old city), the big bonfires, and the illuminations that rang and roared and boomed and burned from Delaware to Schuylkill.

In the waning light of the latest bonfire, up from the city of Penn, rode our Blue-Eyed Boy— true to his purpose to be the first to carry the glad news to General Washington.

"It will be like meeting an old friend," he

thought; for had he not seen the commander-in-chief every day going in and out of the Congress Hall during his visit to Philadelphia only a month ago?

The self-appointed courier never deemed other evidence of the truth of his news needful than his own "word of mouth." He rode a strong young horse, which, early in the year, had been left in his care by a southern officer when on his way to the camp at Cambridge; and that no one might worry about him, he had taken the precaution to intrust his secret to a neighbor lad to tell at the home-door in the light of early day.

The journey was long, too long to write of here. Suffice it to say, that on Sunday morning Blue-Eyed Boy reached the ferry at the Hudson river. The old ferryman hesitated to cross with the lad.

"Wait at my house until the cool of the evening," he urged.

But Blue-Eyed Boy said, "No, I must cross this morning, and my pony: I'll pay for two if you'll take me."

The ferryman crossed the river with the boy, who, on the other side, inquired his way to the headquarters of the general.

Warm, tired, hungry, and dusty, he urged his pony forward to the place, only to find that he whom he sought had gone to divine service at St. Paul's church.

Blue-Eyed Boy rode to St. Paul's. In the

Fields (now City Hall Park) he tied his faithful horse, and went his way to the church.

Gently and with reverent mien, he entered the open door, and listened to the closing words of the sermon. At length the service was over and the congregation turned toward the entrance where stood the young traveler, his heart beating with exultant pride at the glorious news he had to tell to the glorious commander.

How grand the General looked to the boy, as, with stately step, he trod slowly the church aisle accompanied by his officers.

Now he was come to the vestibule. It was Blue-Eyed Boy's chance at last. The great, dancing, gleeful eyes, that have outlived in fame the very name of the lad, were fixed on Washington, as he stepped forward to accost him.

"Out of the way!" exclaimed a guard, and thrust him aside.

"I *will* speak! General Washington!" screamed Blue-Eyed Boy, in sudden excitement. The idea of anybody who had seen, even through a keyhole, the signing of the Declaration of Independence, being thrust aside thus!

General Washington stayed his steps and ordered, "Let the lad come to me."

"I've good news for you," said the youth.

"What news?"

Officers stood around—even the congregation paused, having heard the cry.

"It's for you alone, General Washington."

The lad's eyes were ablaze now. All the light of Philadelphia's late illuminations burned in them. General Washington bade the youth follow him.

"But my pony is tied yonder," said he, "and he's hungry and tired too. I can't leave him."

"Come hither, then," and the Commander-in-chief withdrew with the lad within the sacred edifice.

"General Washington," said Blue-Eyed Boy, "on Thursday Congress declared *us* free and independent."

"Where are your dispatches?" leaped from the General's lips, his face shining.

"Why—why, I haven't any, but it's all true, sir," faltered the boy.

"How did you find it out?"

"I was right there, sir. Don't you remember me? I help Bellman Grey take care of the State House at Philadelphia, and I run on errands for the Congress folks, too, sometimes."

"Did Congress send you on this errand?"

"No, General Washington; I can't tell a lie, I came myself."

"How did you know me?"

Blue-Eyed Boy was ready to cry now. To be sure he was sturdy and strong, and nearly fourteen, too; but to be doubted, after all his long, tiresome journey, was hard. However, he winked once or twice violently, and then he looked his very soul into the General's face, and said: "Why,

I saw you every day you went to Congress, only a month ago, I did."

" I believe you, my lad. Get your horse and follow me."

Bue-Eyed Boy followed on, and waited in camp until the tardy despatches came in on Tuesday morning, confirming every word that he had spoken.

The same evening all the brigades in and around New York were ordered to their respective parade-grounds.

Blue-Eyed Boy was admitted within the hollow square formed by the brigades on the spot where stands the City Hall. Within the same square was General Washington, sitting on horseback, and the great Declaration was read by one of his aids.

It is needless to tell how it was received by the eager men who listened to the mighty truths with reverent, uncovered heads. Henceforth every man felt that he had a banner under which to fight, as broad as the sky above him, as sheltering as the homely roof of home.

THE OVERTHROW OF THE STATUE
OF KING GEORGE.

IF, on the evening of July 9, 1876, at six of the clock, you go and stand where the shadow of the steeple of St. Paul's church in New York is falling, you will occupy the space General Washington occupied, just one hundred years ago, when with uncovered head and reverent mien, he, in the presence of and surrounded by a brigade of noble soldiers, listened to the reading of the Declaration of Independence.

You will remember that at the church door on Sunday, Blue-Eyed Boy brought to him, by word of mouth, the great news that a nation was born on Thursday.

This news was now, for the first time, announced to the men of New York and New England.

No wonder that their military caps came off on Tuesday, that their arms swung in the air, and their voices burst forth into one loud acclaim that might have been heard by the British foe then landing on Staten Island.

As you stand there, and the shadow of old St. Paul swings around and covers you, shut your eyes and listen.   Something of the olden music, of the loud acclaim, may swing around with the shadow and fall on your ears, since no motion is ever spent, no sound ever still.   .

On that night, when the grand burst of enthusiasm had arisen, Blue-Eyed Boy said to General Washington: " I am afraid, sir, if Congress had known, they never would have done it, never! It seemed easy to do it in Philadelphia, where everything is just as it used to be ; but here, with all the British ships riding in, full of soldiers, and guns enough in them to smash the old State House where they did it!   If they'd only known about the ships !—"

Ah! Blue-Eyed Boy.   You didn't keep your eye very close to Congress Hall in the morning of last Thursday, or you would have heard Mr. Hancock or Mr. Thompson read to Congress a letter from General Washington, announcing the arrival of General Howe at Sandy Hook with one hundred and ten ships of war.

No, no! Blue-Eyed Boy and every other boy ; the men who dared to say, and sign their names to the assertion, " A nation is born to-day," did not do it under the rosy flush of glorious victory, but in the fast-coming shadow of mighty Britain, strong in all the power and radiant with all the pomp of war.

And what had a few little colonies to meet them with ?   They had, it is true, a new name, that of " States" ; but cannon and camp-kettles alike were wanting; the small powder mills in the Connecticut hive could yield them only a fragment of the black honey General Washington cried for, day and night, from Cambridge to New York; the houses of the inhabitants, diligently searched for fragments of lead, gave them not enough; and you know how every homestead in New England was besieged for the last yard of homespun cloth, that the country's soldiers might not go coatless by day and tentless at night.

Brave men and women good!

Let us hurrah for them all, if it is a hundred years too late for them to hear. The men of a hundred years to come will remember our huzzas of this year, and grow, it may be, the braver and the better for them all.

But now General Washington has ridden away to his home at Number One in the Broadway; the brigade has moved on, and even Blue-Eyed Boy is hastening after General Washington, intent on taking a farewell glance, from the rampart of Fort George, at the far-away English ships.

To-morrow he will begin his homeward journey through the Jerseys. His pass is in his pocket, and as he quickens his steps, he sees groups gathering here and there, and knows that some excitement is astir in the public mind, but thinks it is all about the great Declaration.

He reaches Wall street, and the sun is at its going down. Up from the East river come the

sounds of orderly drummers drumming, of regi-
mental fifers fifing.   He stays his steps, and
stands listening : he sees a brigade marching the
"grand parade" at sunset.

Up it comes from Wall street to Smith street ;
(I am sure I do not know what Smith street is
lost into now, but the orderly-book of Major
Phineas Porter of Waterbury, one hundred years
old to-morrow morning, has it "Smith street");
from the upper end of Smith street back to Wall
street, and the young Philadelphian follows it,
marching to sound of fife and drum.

As it turns towards the East river, he remembers whither he was bound and starts off with
speed for the Grand Battery. ·

As he goes, glancing backward, he sees that all
the town is at his heels.

He begins to run.   All the town begins to run.
He runs faster : the crowd runs faster.   It is
shouting now.   He tries to listen; but his feet are
flying, his head is bobbing, his hat is falling, and
this is what he thinks he hears in the midst of
all : "Down with him !   Down with the Tory !"
It is "tyrant" that they cry, but he hears it as
"tory," and he knows full well how Governor
Franklin of New Jersey and Mayor Matthews of
New York have just been sent off to Connecticut
for safer keeping, and he does not care to go into
New England just now, so he flies faster than
ever, fully believing that the crowd pursues him,
as a Royalist.

Just before him opens the Bowling Green. Into it he darts, hoping to find covert, but there is none at hand.

Right in the midst of the enclosure stands an equestrian statue of King George the Third.

It is high; it looks safe.   Blue-Eyed Boy makes for it, utterly ignorant of what it is.

The crowd surges on.   It is now at the gate. The young martyr makes a spring at the leg and tail of the horse; he swings himself aloft, he catches and clutches and climbs, and in the midst of ringing shouts of "Down with him! Down with horse and king!" Blue-Eyed Boy gets over King George and clings to the up-reared neck of the leaden horse; thence he turns his wild-eyed face to the throng below.   "Down with him!   He don't hear!   He won't hear!" cry the populace.

"I do hear!" in wild afright, shrieks Blue-Eyed Boy, and I'm not a Tory."

Shut your eyes again, and see the picture as it stands there in the waning light of the ninth of July, 1776.

Four years ago, over the ocean, borne by loyal subjects to a loyal colony, it came, this statue, that you shall see.   It is a noble horse, though made of lead, that stands there, poised on its hinder legs, its neck in air.   King George sits erect, the crown of Great Britain on his head, a sword in his left hand, his right grasping the bridle-lines, and over all, a sheen of gold, for horse and king were gilded.

King George faces the bay, and looks vainly down. All his brave ships and eight thousand Red Coats, yesterday landed on yonder island, cannot save him now. Had he listened to the petitions of his children it might have been, but he would not hear their just plaints, and now his statue, standing so firm against storm, wind and time, trembles before the sea of wrath surging at its base.

"Come down, come down, you young rascal!" cries a strong voice to Blue-Eyed Boy, but his hands grasped at either ear of the horse, and he clings with all his strength to resist the pull of a dozen hands at his feet.

"Come down, you rogue, or we'll topple you over with his majesty, King George," greets the lad's ears, and opens them to his situation.

"King George!" cried Blue-Eyed Boy with a sudden sense of his ridiculous fear and panic, and he yields to the stronger influence exerted on his right leg, and so comes to earth with emotions of relief and mortification curiously mingled in his young mind.

To think that he had had the vanity to imagine the crowd pursued him, and so has flown from his own friends to the statue of King George for safety!

"I won't tell," thinks the lad, "a word about this to anyone at home," and then he falls to pushing the men who are pushing the statue, and over it topples, horse and rider, down upon the sod of the little United States, just five days old.

How they hew it! How they hack it! How they saw at it with saw and penknife! Blue-Eyed Boy himself cuts off the king's ear, that will not hear the petitions of people or Congress, proudly pockets it, and walks off, thankful because he carries his own on his head.

Would you like to know what General Washington thought about the overthrow of the statue in Bowling Green?

We will turn to Phineas Porter's orderly-book, and copy from the general orders for July 10, 1776, what he said to the soldiers about it:

"The General doubts not the persons who pulled down and mutilated the statue in the Broad-way last night were actuated by zeal in the public cause, yet it has so much the appearance of riot and want of order in the army, that he disapproves the manner and directs that in future such things shall be avoided by the soldiers, and be left to be executed by proper authority."

The same morning, the heavy ear of the king in his pocket, Blue-Eyed Boy, once more on his pony, sets off to cross the ferry on his way to Philadelphia. We leave him caught in the mazes of the Flying Camp gathering at Amboy; whither by day and by night have been ferried over from Staten Island, all the flocks of sheep and herds of cattle that could be gotten away—

lest the hungry men in red coats, coming up the bay, seize upon and destroy them.

Ah ! what days, what days and nights too were those for the young United States to pass through !

To-day, we echo what somebody wrote somewhere, even then, amid all the darkness—words we would gladly see on our banner's top-most fold :

" The United States ! Bounded by the ocean and backed by the forest. Whom hath she to fear but her God ?"

SLEET AND SNOW.

OURTH OF JULY, 1776.—Troublous times, that day? Valentine Kull thought so, as he stood in a barn-yard, with a portion of his mother's clothes line tied as tightly as he dared to tie it around the neck of a calf. He was waiting for the bars to be let down by his sister. Anna Kull thought the times decidedly troublous, as she pulled and pushed and lifted to get the bars down.

"I can't do it, Valentine," she cried, her half-child face thrust between the rails.

"Try again!"

She tried. Result as before.

"Come over, then, and hold Snow."

Anna went over, rending gown and apron on the roughnesses of rails and haste. Never mind. She was over, and could, she thought, hold the calf.

Barn-yard, cow (I forgot to mention that there was a cow); calf, and children, one and all, were on Staten Island in the Bay and Province of New York. Beside these, there was a house. It was so small, so queer, so old-fashioned, so Amsterdam Dutchy, that, for all that I know to the contrary, Achter Kull may have built it as a playhouse for his children when first he came to

America and took up his abode by the Kill van
Kull. The Kill van Kull is that curious little
slice of sea pinched in by a finger of New Jersey
thrust hard against Staten Island, as though trying its best to push the island off to sea. However it may have been, there was the house, and
from the very roof of it arose a head, neck, two
shoulders and one arm; the same being the
property of the mother of Valentine and Anna.
The said mother was keeping watch from the
scuttle.

"Be quick, my children," she cried. "The
Continentals are now driving off Abraham Ryker's
cattle and the boat isn't full yet. They'll be *here*
next."

Anna seized the clothes line; Valentine made
for the bars. Down they came, the one after the
other, and out over the lower one went calf, Anna
and cow. Valentine made a dive for Snow's leading string. He missed it. Away went the calf,
poor Anna clutching at the rope, into green lane,
through tall grass, tangle and thicket. She caught
her foot in her torn gown and was falling, when a
sudden holding up of the rope assisted by Valentine's clutch at her arm set her on her feet again.
During this slight respite from the chase, the cow
(Sleet, by name, because not quite so white as
Snow) took a bite of grass and wondered what
all this unaccustomed fuss did mean.

"Snow has pulled my arm out of joint," said
Anna, holding fast to her shoulder.

"Never mind your arm, *now*," returned Valentine. "We must get to the marsh. It's the only place. You get a switch, and if Sleet won't follow Snow in, you drive her. I *wish* the critters wasn't white; they show up so; but Washington sha'n't have this calf and cow, *anyhow.*"

From Newark Bay to Old Blazing Star Ferry stretched the marsh, deep, dense, well-nigh impassable. Under the orders of General Washington, supported by the approval of the Provincial Congress in session at White Plains, the live stock was being driven from the island, and ferried across Staten Island Sound to New Jersey. At the same moment the grand fleet of armed ships from Halifax, England, and elsewhere, was sailing in with General Howe on board and Red Coats enough to eat, at a supper and a dinner, all the live stock on a five-by-seventeen mile island.

Now the Commander-in-chief of the Continental forces at New York did not wish to afford the aid and comfort to the enemy of furnishing horses to draw cannon, or fresh meat wherewith to satisfy the hunger of British soldier and sailor. Oh no! On Manhattan Island were braves—for freedom toiling day and night; building earthwork, redoubt and battery with never a luxury from morning to morning, except the luxury of fighting for Liberty. Soldiers from camp, light-horse and militia from New Jersey, had gathered on the island, and had been at work a day and a night when the news came to the Kull cottage that in a

10

few minutes its cow and calf would be called for. Hence the sudden watch from the roof, and the escapade from the barn-yard.

The Kull father, I regret to write, because it seems highly unpatriotic, had gone forth to catch fish that day, hugging up the thought close to his pocket of a heart, that the English fleet would pay well for fresh fish.

Now Sleet and Snow were treasures untold to Valentine and Anna Kull. Anna's pocket-money, stored up to be spent once-a-year in New York, came to her hands by the sale of butter to oyster-men; and the calf, Snow, was the exclusive property of her brother Valentine. No wonder they were striving to save their possessions— ignorant, children as they were, of every good which they could not see and feel.

Cow and calf, or rather calf and cow, never before were given such a race. Highways were ignored. There were not many beaten tracks at that time on Staten Island. Daisied and clovered fields the calf was dragged through; young corn and potato lots suffered alike by the pressure of hoof and foot. Anna nearly forgot her out-of-joint arm when the four reached the marsh. Its friendly-looking shelter was hailed with delight.

Said Valentine, tugging the tired calf, to Anna, switching forward the anxious cow: "I should like to see the riflemen from Pennsylvania and the *Yankeys* from Doodle or Dandy either, chase Sleet and Snow through *this* marsh."

" It's been *awful* work though to get 'em here,"
said Anna, wiping her face with a pink handker-
chief suddenly detached for use from her gown.

In plunged the boy and up s-s-cissed a cloud of
mosquitoes, humming at the sound of the new-
come feast ; fresh flesh and blood from the up-
lands was desirable.

The grass was green, *very* green—lovely, bright,
light green ; the July sun shone down untiringly ;
the tide rushing up from Raritan Bay met the'
tide rolling over from Newark Bay, and the cool,
sweet swash of water snaked along the stout
sedge, making it sway and bend as though the
wind were sweeping its tops.

When within the queer infolding, boy, cow, and
calf had disappeared, Anna called : " I'll run now
and keep watch and tell you when the soldiers
are gone."

" No, *you won't !* " shrieked back her brother ;
" you'll stay *here*, and help me, or the skeeters
will kill the critters. Bring me the biggest bush
you can find, and fetch one for yourself."

Anna always obeyed Valentine. It was a way
she had. He liked it, and, generally speaking,
she didn't greatly dislike it, but her dress was
thinner than his coat, and the happy mosquitoes
knew she was fairer and sweeter than her Dutch
brother, and didn't mind telling her so in the
most insinuating fashion possible. On this occasion, as she had in so many other unlike instances,
she acceded to his request; toiling backward up

the ascent and fetching thence an armful of the stoutest boughs she could twist from branches.

She neared the marsh on her return. All that she could discern was a straw hat bobbing hither and thither; the horns of a cow tossing to and fro; the tail of a cow lashing the air.

A voice she heard, shouting forth in impatient bursts of sound, "Anna, Anna Kull!"

"*Here!* I'm coming," she responded.

"Hurry up! I'm eaten alive. Snow's crazy and Sleet's a lunatic," shouted her brother, jerking the words forth between the vain dives his hand made into the cloud of wings in the air.

"Sakes alive!" said poor Anna, toiling from sedge bog to sedge bog with her burden of "bushes" and striving to hide her face from the mosquitoes as she went.

It was nearly noon-day then, and the Fourth of July too, but neither Valentine nor Anna thought of the day of the month. Why should they? The Nation wasn't born yet whose hundredth birthday we keep this year.

The solemn assembly of earnest men—debating the to be or not to be of the United States—was over there at work in Congress Hall in the old State House. They were heated with sun and brick and argument; a hundred and ten British ships of war were anchoring and at anchor over on the ocean side of Staten Island. Up the bay, seven or eight thousand troops in "ragged regimentals" were working to make ready for battle;

but not one of them all suffered more from sun and toil and anxiety and greed of blood than did the lad and the lass in the marsh.

They fought it out, with many a sting and smart, another hour, and then declaring that "cow of no cow they couldn't stay another minute," they strove to work their way out of the beautiful green of the sedge.

On the meadow-land stood their mother. She had brought dinner for her hungry children,— moreover, she had brought news.

The Yankee troops—the Jersey militia—had gone, but the British soldiers had arrived and demanded beef—beef raw, beef roasted, beef in any form.

The tears that the fiercest mosquito had failed to extort from Anna came now. "I wish I'd let her go," she cried, fondly stroking Sleet. At least she wouldn't have been killed, and we'd had her again sometime, maybe; but now—I say, Valentine, are *you* going to give up Snow?"

"No, I *ain't*," stoutly persisted the lad, slapping with his broad palm the panting side of the calf, where mosquitoes still clung.

"But, my poor children," said Mother Kull, "you will *have* to. It *can't* be helped. If we refuse them, don't you know, they will burn our house down."

"*If they do, I'll kill them!*" The words shot out from the gunpowdery temper of Anna Kull. Poor innocent girl of thirteen! She never in her

life had seen an act of cruelty greater than the
taking of a fish or the death of a chicken ; but the
impotent impulse of revenge arose within her at
the bare idea of having her pet, her pretty Sleet,
taken from her and eaten by soldiers.

"You'd better keep still, Anna Kull," said
Valentine. "Mother, don't you think we might
hide the animals somewhere?"

"Where?" echoed the poor woman, looking
up and looking down.

Truly there seemed to be no place. Already
six thousand British soldiers had landed and taken
possession of the island. Hills and forests were
not high enough nor deep enough ; and now the
very marsh had cast them out by its army of
winged stingers—more dreadful than human foe.

"I just wish," ejaculated the poor sunburned,
mosquito-tortured, hungry girl, who stood between marsh and meadow,—"I *wish* I had 'em
every one tied hand and foot and dumped into
the sedge where we've been. Mother, I wouldn't
use Sleet's milk to-night, not a drop of it,—it's
crazy milk, I know: she's been tortured so. Poor
cow! poor creature! poor, dear, nice, honest
Sleet!" And Anna patted the cow with loving
stroke and laid her head on its neck.

"Well, children, eat something, and then we'll
all go home together,—if they haven't carried off
our cot already," said the mother.

They sat down under a tree and ate with the
eager, wholesome appetite of children.   Mrs.

Kull kept watch that the cow did not wander far from the place.

As they were eating, Valentine said to Anna, nodding his head in the direction of his mother: "I've thought of something. We must manage to send *her* home without us."

"*I've* thought of something," responded Anna. "Yes, we *must* manage."

"I should like to know *what* you could think of, sister."

"Should you? Why, think of saving the cow and calf, of course; though, if you're *very* particular, you can leave the calf here."

"And what will you do with the cow?"

"Put her in the boat—"

"Whew!" interrupted Valentine.

"And ferry her over the sound," continued Anna.

"Who?"

"You and me."

"Do you think we could?"

"We can try."

"That's brave! How's your arm?"

"All right! I jerked it back, slapping mosquitoes."

"Give us another hunkey piece of bread and butter. Honey's good to-day. I wonder mother thought about it."

"I s'pose," said Anna, "she'd as leave we had it as soldiers. Wouldn't it be jolly if we could make 'em steal the bees?"

The wind blew east. Up came martial sounds mingled with the break and the roar of the ocean.

"Oh, dear! They're a coming," gasped Mrs. Kull, running to the spot. "They're coming, and your father is not here."

"Hide, hide, my children! Never mind the cow now," she almost shrieked; her mind was running wild with all the scenes of terror she had ever heard of.

"Pshaw! pshaw! Mother Kull," said her boy, assuringly. "They won't come down here. Somebody's guiding them around who knows just where every house is. You and Anna get into that thicket yonder and keep, whatever happens, as still as mice."

"What'll *you* do, bub?" questioned Anna, her sunburned face brown-pale with affright.

"Oh, I'll take care of myself. Boys always do."

As soon as Mrs. Kull and her daughter were well concealed in the thicket, the sounds began to die away. They waited half an hour. All was still. They crept out, gazing the country over. No soldier in sight. Down in the marsh again were boy and cow.

"I'll run home now," said Mrs. Kull. I dare say 'twas all a trick of my ears."

"But I heard it, too, Mother Kull."

"Your ears serve you tricks, too, Anna. You wait and help Valentine home with the animals."

Anna was glad to have her mother gone. She sped to the marsh. She threaded it, until by sundry signs she found the trio and summoned them forth.

The old Blazing Star Ferry was seldom used. A boat lay there. It was staunch. The tide with them, they *might* get it across. Had they been older, wiser, they would never have made the attempt.

A fresh water stream ran down to the sea. They passed it on their way thither. In it Sleet drank deep, and soothed for a moment the bites that tormented her; the children kneeled on the grassy bank, and drank from their palms; the calf frolicked in it, till driven out. An hour went by. They reached the ferry. It was deserted. Somebody had used the boat that day. It was at the shore. Grass was yet in it.

"Come along, Snow," said Valentine, urging with the rope. "Go along, Snow," said Anna, helping it on with a stout twig she had picked up. The calf pranced and ran, and before it knew its whereabouts was in the broad-bottomed boat. Sleet stood on the shore, and saw her baby tied fast. One poor cry the calf uttered. It went home to the motherly heart of the dumb creature. She went down the sand, over the side, and began, in her own way, to comfort Snow.

"Now we are all right!" cried Valentine, delighted with the success of his ruse; for he had slyly, lest Anna should see the deed, thrust a pin in Snow to call forth the cry and win the cow over to his side.

"Take an oar quick!" commanded the young captain.

His mate obeyed. They pushed the boat out, unfastened it from the pier. Before anybody concerned had time to realize the situation the boat was adrift, and they were whirling in the tide.

"Now, sis," said Valentine, a big lump in his throat, "we're in for it. It is sink or swim. It's not much use to row. You steer and I'll paddle."

Sleet looked wildly around. She tossed her head, sniffed the salt, oystery air, and seemed about to plunge overboard.

Anna screamed. Valentine threw down his paddle and dashed himself on the boat's outermost edge just in time to save it from overturning. Mistress Sleet, disgusted with Fourth of July, had made up her mind to lie down and take a nap. The boat righted and they were safe. Staten Island Sound at this point was narrow, scarcely more than a quarter of a mile in width, and the tide was fast bearing them out.

"Such uncommon good sense in Sleet," exclaimed the boy. "*That* cow is worth saving."

At that moment a dozen Red Coats were at the ferry they had just left. The imperious gentlemen were in a fine frenzy at finding the boat gone.

They shouted to the children to return.

"Steady, steady now," cried the young captain. His mate was steady at the helm until a musket ball or two ran past them.

"Let go!" shouted the captain. "Swing your

bonnet. Let them know you're a woman and they won't fire on *you*."

The little mate stood erect. She waved her pink flag of a sun-bonnet. Distinctly the soldiers saw the pink frock of Anna Kull; they saw her long hair as the sea breeze lifted it when she shook her pink banner.

A second, two, three went by as the girl stood there, and then a flash was seen on the bank, a musket-ball ran through the bonnet of the little mate, and the waves of air rattled along the shore.

The bonnet was in the sea; Anna had dropped to her seat and caught the helm in her left hand.

"Cowards!" cried Valentine, for want of a stronger word, and then he fell to working the boat on its way. The tide helped them now; it swung the boat over toward the Jersey shore.

The firing from Staten Island called out the inhabitants on the Jersey coast. They watched the approaching boat with interest. Everything depended now on the cow's lying still, on the boy's strength, on the meeting of the tides. If he could reach there before the tide came up all would be well; otherwise it would sweep him off again toward the island.

" Can't you row?" asked Valentine, at length.

" Bub, I can't," said Anna, her voice shaking out the words. It was the first time she had spoken since she sat down.

" Are you hurt?" he questioned.

"I tremble so," she answered, and turned her face away.

"I reckon we'd better help that boy in," said a Jersey fisherman as he watched, and he put off in a small boat.

"Don't come near! Keep off! keep off!" called Valentine, as he saw him approach. "I've a cow in here."

The fisherman threw him a rope, and that rope saved them. The dewy smell of the grassy banks had aroused the cow. She was stirring.

The land was very near now; close at hand. "Hurry! hurry!" urged the lad, as they were drawing him in. Before the cow had time to rise, the boat touched land.

"You'd better look after that girl," said the fisherman, who had towed the boat. The poor child was holding, fast wrapped in the remnants of her pink frock, her bleeding hand. The musket ball that shot away her bonnet grazed her wrist.

"Never mind me," she said, when they were pitying her. "The cow is safe."

The same evening, while, in Philadelphia, bonfires were blazing, bells ringing, cannon booming, because, that day, a new nation was born; over Staten Island Sound, by the light of the moon, strong-armed men were ferrying home the girl and the boy, who that day *had* fought a good fight and gained the victory.

At home, in the Kull cottage, the mother

waited long for the coming of the children. She said; "Poor young things! *Mine own children—* they *shall* have a nice supper." She made it ready and they were not come.

Farmer Rycker's wife and daughter came over to tell and hear the news, and yet they were not come.

Sundown. No children. The Kull father came up from his fishing and heard the story.

"The Red Coats have taken them," he said, and down came the musket from against the wall, and out the father marched and made straightway for the headquarters of General Howe, over at the present "Quarantine."

Then the mother, left alone in the soft summer gloaming, fell on her knees and told her story in her own plain speech to her good Father in Heaven.

It was a long story. She had much to say to Heaven that night. The mothers and wives of 1776 in our land spake often unto God. This mother listened and prayed, and prayed and listened.

The fishermen had left Valentine and Anna on the shore and gone home. Tired, but happy, the brother and sister went up, over sand and field and slope, and so came at length within sight of the trees that towered near home.

"Whistle now!" whispered Anna, afraid yet to speak aloud. "Mother will hear and answer."

Valentine whistled.

Up jumped the mother Kull. She ran to the door and tried to answer. There was no whistle in her lips. Joy choked it.

"Mother, are you *there?*" cried the children.

"No! I'm *here*," was the answer, and she had them safe in her arms.

Patty Rutter: The Quaker Doll who slept in Independence Hall.

———

ATTY RUTTER had fallen asleep with her bonnet on, and had been lying there, fast asleep, nobody knew just how long; for, somehow—it happened so—there was nobody in particular to awaken her; that is to say, no one had seemed to care though she slept on all day and all night, without ever waking up at all.

But then, there never had been another life quite like Patty Rutter's life. In the first place, it had a curious reason for beginning at all; and nearly everything about it had been as unlike your life and mine as possible.

In her very baby days, before she walked or talked, she had been sent away to live with strangers, and no real, warm kiss of true love had ever fallen on her little lips.

It all came about in this way: Mrs. Sarah Rutter, a lady living in Philadelphia—exactly what relation she bore to Patty it is a little difficult to determine—decided to send the little one to live with a certain Mrs. Adams, at Quincy, in Massachusetts, and she particularly desired that the child should go dressed in a style fitting an inhabitant of the proud city of Philadelphia.

Now, at that time Philadelphia was very much elated because of several things that had happened to her; but the biggest pride of all was, that once upon a time the Continental Congress had met there, and—and most wonderful thing— had made a Nation !

Well, to be sure, that *was* something to be proud of; though Patty didn't understand, a bit more than you do, what it meant. However, the glory of it all was talked about so much that she couldn't help knowing that, when this nation, with its fifty-six Fathers, and thirteen Mothers, was born one day in July, 1776, at Philadelphia, all the city rang with a sweet jangle, and called to all the people, through the tongue of its Liberty bell, to come up and greet the new-comer with a great shout of welcome.

But that had been long ago, before Mrs. Sarah Rutter was grown up, or Patty Rutter began to be dressed for her trip to Quincy.

As I wrote, Mrs. Rutter wished that Patty should go attired in a manner to do honor to the city of Philadelphia; therefore she was not permitted to depart in her baby clothes, but her little figure was arrayed in a long, prim gown of soft drab silk, while a kerchief of purest mull was crossed upon her breast; and, depending from her waist, like the fashion of to-day, were pin-cushion and watch. Upon her youthful head

was a bonnet, crowned and trimmed in true
Quaker fashion; and her infantile feet were
securely tied within shapely slippers of kid.
Thus equipped, Miss Patty was sent forth upon
her journey.

Ah! that journey began a long time ago—fifty-
eight, yes, fifty-nine years have gone by, and
Patty Rutter is quite an aged little lady now, as
she lies asleep, with her bonnet on.

" It is time," says somebody, " to close."

No one seems to take notice that Patty Rutter
does not get up and depart with the rest of the
visitors, that she only stirs her eyelids and turns
her head on the silken "quilt" where she is
lying.

The little woman who keeps house in the Hall
locks it up and goes away, and there is little
Patty Rutter shut in for the night. As the key
turns in the old-time lock, the Lady Rutter winks
hard and sits up.

" Well, I've been patient, anyhow, and Mrs.
Samuel Adams herself couldn't wish me to do
more," she said, with a comforting yawn and a
delightful stretch, and then she began to stare in
blank bewilderment.

" I *should* like to know what this all means," she
whispered, "and *where* I am. I've heard enough
to-day to turn my head. How very queer folks
are, and they talk such jargon now-a-days. Centennial and Corliss Engine; Woman's Pavilion
and Memorial Hall; Main Building and the

Trois Freres; Hydraulic Annex, railroads and what-nots.

"*I* never heard of such things. I don't think it is proper to speak of them, or the Adamses would have told me. No more intelligent folks in the land than the Adamses, and I guess *they* know what belongs to good society and polite conversation. I declare I blushed so in my sleep that I was quite ashamed. I'll get up and look about now. I'm sure this isn't any one of the houses where we visit, or folks wouldn't talk so."

Patty Rutter straightened her bonnet on her head, smoothed down her robe of silken drab, adjusted her kerchief, looked at her watch to learn how long she had been sleeping, and found, to her surprise, that it had run down. Right over her head hung two watches.

" Why, how thoughtful folks are in this house," she exclaimed in a timid voice, reaching up and taking one of the two time-pieces in her hand. " Why, here's a name ; let me see."

Reading slowly, she announced that the watch belonged to " Wil-liam Wil-liams—worn when he signed the Declaration of Independence." " Ah !" she cried, with pathetic tone, " this watch is run down *too*, at four minutes after five. I remember ! *This* William Williams was one of the fifty-six Fathers. I guess I must be in Lebanon—he lived there and his folks would have his watch of course. Here's another," taking down a watch and reading, " Colonel John Trumbull. *Run*

down, too! and at twenty-three minutes after six.
He was the son of Brother Jonathan, Governor
of one of the Mothers, when the Nation was born.
Yes, yes, I must be in Lebanon. Well, it's a comfort, at least, to know that I'm in company the
Adamses would approve of, though *how* I came
here is a mystery."

She hung the watches in place, stepped out of
the glass room, in which she had slept, into a hall,
and with a slight exclamation of delicious approval, stopped short before a number of chairs,
and clasped her little fingers tightly together.

You must remember that Patty Rutter was a
Friend, a Quaker, perhaps a descendant of William Penn, but then, in her baby days, having
been transplanted to the rugged soil and out-
spoken ways of Massachusetts, she could not
keep silence altogether, in view of that which
greeted her vision.

She was in the very midst of old friends.
Chairs in which she had sat in her young days
stood about the grand hall. On the walls hung
portraits of the ancestor kings of the nation born
at Philadelphia in 1776.

In royal robes and with careless grace, lounged
King George III., the nation's grandfather, angry
no longer at his thirteen daughters who strayed
from home with the Sons of Liberty.

Her feet made haste and her eyes opened
wider, as her swift hands seized relic after relic.
She sat in chairs that Washington had rested in

she caught up camp-kettles used on every field
where warriors of the Revolution had tarried;
she patted softly La Fayette's camp bedstead;
and wondered at the taste that had put into the
hall two old, time-worn, battered doors, but soon
found out that they had gone through all the
storm of balls that fell upon the Chew House
during the battle of Germantown.

She read the wonderful prayer that once was
prayed in Carpenter's Hall, and about which
every member of Congress wrote home to his
wife.

On a small " stand," encased in glass, she came
upon a portrait of Washington, painted during
the time he waited for powder at Cambridge.
Patty Rutter had seen it often, with its halo of
the General's own hair about it. She turned
from it, and beheld (why, yes, surely she *had* seen
that, but not here; it was, why long ago, in her
baby days in Philadelphia, that Mrs. Rutter had
taken her up into a tower to see it, a bell—
Liberty Bell, that rang above the heads of the
Fathers when the Nation was born.

Poor little Patty began to cry. Where could
she be? She reached out her hand, and climbed
the huge beams that encased the bell, and tried
to touch the tongue. She wanted to hear it ring
again, but could not reach it.

" It's curious, curious," she sobbed, wiping her
eyes and turning them with a thrill of delight
upon a beloved name that greeted her vision. It

was growing dark, and she *might* be wrong. But
no, it was the dear name of Adams; and she saw,
in a basket, a little pile of baby raiment. There
were dainty caps and tiny shirts of cambric,
whose linen was like a gossamer web, and whose
delicate lines of hem-stitch were scarcely dis-
cernible; there were small dresses, yellow with
the sun color that time had poured over them,
and they hung with pathetic crease and tender
fold over the sides of the basket.

The little woman paused and peered to read
these words, "Baby-clothes, made by Mrs. John
Adams for her son, John Quincy Adams."

"Little John Quincy!" she cried, "A baby so
long ago!" She took the little caps in her hands,
she pulled out the crumpled lace that edged
them. She said, through the swift-falling tears:

"Oh, I remember when he was brought home
dead, and how, in the Independence Hall of the
State House at Philadelphia, he lay in state, that
the inhabitants who knew his deeds, and those of
his father, John, and his uncle, Samuel, might
see his face. I love the Adamses every one," and
she softly pressed the baby-caps that had been
wrought by a mother, ere the country began, to
her small Quaker lips, with real New England
fervor for its very own. Tenderly she laid them
down, to see, while the light was fading, a huge
picture on the wall. She studied it long, trying
to discern the faces, with their savage beauty;
the sturdy right-doing men who stood before

them; and then her eyes began to glisten, and gather light from the picture; her lips parted, her breath quickened; for Patty Rutter had gone beyond her life associations in Massachusetts, back to the times in which her Quaker ancestors had make treaty with the native Indians.

"It is!" she cried with a shout; "It is Penn's treaty!" Patty gazed at it until she could see no longer. "I'm glad it is the last thing my eyes will remember," she said sorrowfully, when in the gloom she turned away, went down the hall, and entered her glass chamber.

"Never mind my watch," she said softly. "When I waken it will be daylight, and I need not wind it. It will be so sweet to lie here through the night in such grand and goodly company. I only wish Mrs. Samuel Adams could come and kiss me good night."

With these words, Patty Rutter laid herself to rest upon the silken quilt from Gardiner's Island; and if you look within the Relic Room, opposite to Independence Hall, in the old State House at Philadelphia, in this Centennial summer, you will find her there, still taking her long nap, *fully indorsed by Miss Adams*, and in Independence Hall, across the passage way, you will see the portraits of more than fifty of the Fathers of the nation, but the Mothers abide at home.

BECCA BLACKSTONE'S TURKEYS AT VALLEY FORGE.

TURKEYS, little girl and apple-tree lived in Pennsylvania, a hundred years ago. The turkeys—eleven of them—went to bed in the apple-tree, one night in December.

After it was dark, the little girl stood under the tree and peered up through the boughs and began to count. She numbered them from one up to eleven. Addressing the turkeys, she said: " You're all up there, I see, and if you only knew enough; if you weren't the dear, old, wise, stupid things that you are, I'll tell you what you would do. After I'm gone in the house, and the door is shut, and nobody here to see, you'd get right down, and you'd fly off in a hurry to the deepest part of the wood to spent your Thanksgiving, you would. The cold of the woods isn't half as bad for you as the fire of the oven will be."

Becca finished her speech; the turkeys rustled in their feathers and doubtless wondered what it all meant, while she stood thinking. One poor fellow lost his balance and came fluttering down to the ground, just as she had decided what to do. As soon as he was safely reset on his perch,

Becca made a second little speech to her audience. in which she declared that "they, the dear turkeys, were her own; that she had a right to do with them just as she pleased, and that it was her good pleasure that not one single one of the eleven should make a part of anybody's Thanksgiving dinner."

"Heigh-ho," whistles Jack, Becca's ten-year-old brother: "that you, Bec? High time you were in the house."

"S'pose I frightened you," said Becca. "Where have you been gone all the afternoon, I'd like to know? stealin' home too, across lots.'

"I'll tell, if you won't let on a mite."

"Do I ever, Jack?" reproachfully.

He did not deign to answer, but in confidential whispers breathed it into her ears that "he had been down to the Forge. Down to the Valley Forge, where General Washington was going to fetch down lots and lots of soldiers, and build log huts, and stay all Winter." He ended his breathless narration with an allusion that made Becca jump as though she had seen a snake. He said: "It will be bad for your turkeys."

"Why, Jack? General Washington won't steal them."

"Soldiers eat turkey whenever they can get it; and, Bec, this apple-tree isn't above three miles from the Forge. You'd better have 'em all killed for Thanksgiving. Come, I'm hungry as a bear."

" But," said Becca, grasping his jacket sleeve as they went, "I've just promised 'em that they shall not be touched."

Jack's laugh set every turkey into motion, until the tree was all in a flutter of excitement. He laughed again and again, before he could say "What a little goose you are! Just as if turkeys understood a word you said."

" But I understood if they didn't, and I should be telling my own self a lie. No, not a turkey shall die. They shall all have a real good Thanksgiving once in their lives."

Two days later, on the 18th of December, Thanksgiving Day came, the turkeys were yet alive, and Becca Blackstone was happy.

The next day General Washington's eleven thousand men marched into Valley Forge, and went out upon the cold, bleak hillsides, carrying with them almost three thousand poor fellows, too ill to march, too ill to build log huts, ill enough to lie down and die. Such a busy time as there was for days and days. Farmer Blackstone felt a little toryish in his thoughts, but the chance to sell logs and split slabs so near home as Valley Forge was not likely to happen again, and he worked away with strong good will to furnish building material. Jack went every day to the encampment, and grew quite learned in the ways of warlike men.

Becca staid at home with her mother, but secretly wished to see what the great army looked like.

At last the final load of chestnut and walnut and oaken logs went up to the hills from Mr. Blackstone's farm, and a great white snow fell down over all Pennsylvania, covering the mountains and hills, the soldiers' log huts, and the turkeys in the apple-tree. January came and went, and every day affairs at the camp grew worse. Men were dying of hunger and cold and disease. Stories of the sufferings of the men grew strangely familiar to the inhabitants. Affairs that Winter would not have been quite so hard at Valley Forge if the neighbors for miles around had not been Tories. Now Becca Blackstone's mother was a New England women, and in secret she bestowed many a comfort upon one after another of her countrymen at the encampment. Her husband was willing to sell logs and slabs and clay from his pits, but not a farthing or a splinter of wood had he to bestow on the rebels.

At last, one January day, when Mr. Blackstone had gone to Philadelphia, permission was given to Becca to accompany her mother and Jack to the village. Into the rear of the sleigh a big basket was packed. Becca was told that she must not ask any questions nor peep, so she neither questioned nor looked in, but found out, after all, for when they were come to the camp, she saw her mother take 'out loaves of rye bread and a jug, into which she knew nothing but milk ever was put, and carry them into a hut which had the sign of a hospital over it. Every third cabin was a hospital, and each and every one held within it men that were always hungry and in suffering.

In all her life Becca had never seen so much to make her feel sorry, as she saw when she followed her mother to the door of the log-hospital, into which she was forbidden to enter.

There large-eyed, hungry men lay on the cold ground, with only poor, wretched blankets to cover them. She caught a glimpse of a youth— he did not seem much older than her own Jack— with light, fair hair, such big blue eyes, and the thinnest, whitest hands, reaching up for the mug of milk her mother was offering to him.

Then, when Jack came to her, he was wiping his eyes on his jacket sleeve. He said "If I was a soldier, and my country didn't care any more for me than Congress does, I'd go home and leave the Red Coats to carry off Congress. It's too bad, and he's a jolly good fellow. Wish we could take him home and get him well."

"Who is he, Jack?"

"O, a soldier-boy from one of the New England colonies. He's got a brother with him—that's good."

The drive home, over the crisp snow, was a very silent one. More than one tear froze on Mrs. Blackstone's cheek, as she remembered the misery her eyes had beheld, and her hands could do so little to lighten.

The next day Mr. Blackstone reached home from Philadelphia. He had seen the Britons in

all the glory and pomp of plenty and red regimentals . in a prosperous city. He returned a
confirmed Tory, and wished—never mind what
he did wish, since his unkind wish never came to
pass—but this is that which he did, he forbade
Mrs. Blackstone to give anything that belonged
to him to a soldier of General Washington's army.

"What will you do now, mamma, with all the
stockings and mittens you are knitting?" questioned Becca.

"Don't ask me, child," was the tearful answer
that mother made, for her whole heart was with
her countrymen in their brave struggle.

Three nights after that time Mr. Blackstone
entered his house, saying :

"I caught a ragged, bare-footed tatterdemalion
hanging around, and I warned him off; told him
he'd better go home, if he'd got one anywhere,
and if not to join the army, of his king at Philadelphia."

"What did he say, pa?" asked Jack.

"O some tomfoolery or other about the man
having nothing to eat but hay for two days, and
his brother dying over at the Forge. I didn't
stop to listen to the fellow, but sent him flying."

Jack touched his mother's toe in passing, and
gave Becca a mysterious nod of the head, as much
as to say :

"He's the soldier from our hospital over there,"
but nobody made answer to Mr. Blackstone.

Becca's eyes filled with tears as she sat down at the tea-table, and sturdy Jack staid away until the last minute, taking all the time he could at washing his hands, that he might get as many looks as possible through the window in the hope that the bare-footed soldier might be lingering about, but he gained no glimpse of him.

Farmer Blackstone had the rheumatism sometimes, and that night he had it worse than ever, so that an hour after tea-time he was quite ready to go to bed, and his wife was quite ready to have him go, also to give him the soothing, quieting remedies he called for.

Becca was to sit up that night until eight-of-the-clock, if she made no noise to disturb her father.

While her mother was busied in getting her father comfortable, she thought, as it was such bright moonlight, she would go out to give her turkeys a count, it having been two or three nights since she had counted them.

Slipping a shawl of her mother's over her head, she opened softly the kitchen door to steal out. The lowest possible whistle from Jack accosted her at the house corner. That lad intercepted her course, drew her back into the shadow, and bade her " Look !"

She looked across the snow, over the garden wall, into the orchard, and there, beneath her apple-tree, stood something between a man and a scarecrow, and it appeared to be looking up at the sleeping turkeys. Both arms were uplifted.

"O dear! what shall we do?" whispered Becca, all in a shiver of cold and excitement.

"Let's go and speak to him. Maybe it is our hospital man," said Jack, with a great appearance of courage.

The two children started, hand in hand, and approached the soldier so quietly that he did not hear the sound of their coming.

As they went, Becca squeezed her brother's fingers and pointing to the snow over which they walked, whispered the word "Blood!"

"From his feet," responded Jack, shutting his teeth tightly together.

Yes, there it lay in bright drops on the glistening snow, showing where the feet of the patriot had trod. The children stood still when they were come near to the tree. At the instant their mother appeared in the kitchen doorway and called "Jack!"

The ragged soldier of the United American States lost his courage at the instant and began to retire in confusion; but Becca summoned him to "Wait a minute!" He waited.

"Did you want one of my turkeys?" she asked.

"I was going to *steal* one, to save my brother's life," he answered.

"Is he only a boy, and has he light hair and blue eyes, and does he lie on the wet ground?"

"That's Joseph," he groaned.

"Then take a good, big, fat turkey—that one there, if you can get him," said Becca. "They are all mine."

The turkey was quietly secured.

"Now take one for yourself," said Becca.

Number two came down from the perch.

"How many men are there in your hospital?" asked Jack, who had responded to his mother's summons, and was holding a pair of warm stockings in his hand.

"Twelve."

"Give him another, Bec—there's a good girl; three turkeys ain't a bone too many for twelve hungry men," prompted Jack.

"Take three!" said Becca. "My pa never counts my turkeys."

The third turkey joined his fellows.

"Better put these stockings on before you start, or father will track you to the camp," said Jack. "And pa told ma never to give you anything of his any more."

Never was weighty burden more cheerfully borne than the bag Jack helped to hoist over the soldier's shoulder as soon as the stockings had been drawn over the bleeding feet.

"Now I'm going. Thank you, and good night. If you, little girl, would give me a kiss, I'd take it—as from my little Bessy in Connecticut."

"That's for Bessy in Connecticut," said the little girl, giving him one kiss, "and now I'll give you one for Becca in Pennsylvania. Hurry home and roast the turkeys quick."

They watched him go over the hill.

" Jack," said Becca, " if I'd told a lie to the turkeys where would they have been to-night, and
Joseph? There are eight more. I wish I'd told
him to come again. Pa's rheumatism came just
right to-night, didn't it?

" I reckon next year you won't have all the
turkeys to give away to the soldiers," said Jack,
adding quite loftily, " I shall go to raising turkeys
in the Spring myself, and when Winter comes we
shall see."

" Now, Jacky," said Becca, half-crying, "there
are eight left, and you take half."

" No, I won't," rejoined Jack. " I'd just like to
walk over to Valley Forge and see the soldiers
enjoy turkey. Won't they have a feast!   I
shouldn't wonder if they'd eat one raw."

" O, Jack!"

"Soldiers do eat dreadful things sometimes,"
he assured her with a lofty air. And then they
went into the house, and the door was shut.

The next year there was not a soldier left above
the sod at Valley Forge.

Now the soldiers are gone, the camp is not, the
little girl has passed away, the apple-tree is dead,
and only the hills at Valley Forge are left to tell
the story, bitter with suffering, eloquent with
praise, of the men who had a hundred years ago
toiled for Freedom there, and are gone home to
God.

HOW TWO LITTLE STOCKINGS
SAVED FORT SAFETY.

"STORY, children; so soon after Christmas, too! Let me think, what shall it be?"

"O yes, mamma," uttered three children in chorus.

Mrs. Livingston sat looking into the fire that flamed on the broad hearth so long, that Carl said, by way of reminder that time was passing: "An uncommon story."

Then up spoke Bessie: "Mamma, something, please, out of the real old time before much of anybody 'round here was born."

"As long off as the Indians," assisted young Dot.

"Ah yes; that will do, children. I will tell you a story that happened in this very house almost a hundred years ago. It was told to me by my grandmother when she was very old."

There was a grand old lady, Mrs. Livingston, at the head of this house then. She loved her country very much indeed, and was willing to do anything she could to help it, in the time of great trouble, during the war for independence. My grandmother was a little girl, not so old as you, Bessie. Her name was Lorinda Grey, and her home was in Boston. The year before, when British soldiers kept close watch to, see that nothing to eat, or wear, or burn, was carried into Boston, Mr. Grey contrived to get his family out of the city, and Lorinda, with her brother Otis, was sent here. Afterward, when Boston was free again, the two children were left because the father was too busy to make the long journey after them.

Altogether, more than a dozen children belonging in some way to the Livingstons had been sent to the old house. The family friends and relatives gave the place the name " Fort Safety," because it lay far away from the enemy's ships, and quite out of the line where the soldiers of either army marched or camped.

The year had been very full of sorrow and care and trouble and hard work; but when the time for Christmas drew near, this grand old Mrs. Livingston said it should be the happiest Christmas that the old house had ever known. She would make the children happy once, whatever might come afterward, and so she set about it quite early in the fall. One day the children (there were more than a dozen of them in the house at the time) found out that the great room at the end of the hall was locked. They asked Mrs. Livingston many times when it meant, and at last she told them that one night after they were in bed and asleep, Santa Claus appeared at her door and asked if he might occupy that room until the night before Christmas. She told him he might, and he had locked the door himself, and said " if any child so much as looked through a crack in the door that child would find nothing but chest-nut burs in his stocking." Well, the children knew that Santa Claus meant what he said, always, so they used to run past the door every day as fast as they could go and keep their eyes the other way, lest something should be seen that ought not to. Before the day came every wide chimney in the house was swept bright and clean for Santa Claus.

Aunt Elise, a sweet young lady, lived here then. She was old Mrs. Livingston's daughter, and she told the children that she had seen Santa Claus with her own eyes when he locked the door, and he said that every room must be made as fine as fine could be.

After that Tom and Richard and Will and Philip worked away as hard as they could. They gathered bushels and bushels of ivy, and a mile or two of ground-pine, and eight or ten pecks of bitter-sweet, and stored them all in the corn granary, and waited for the day. Then, when Aunt Elise set to work to adorn the house, she had twenty-four willing hands to help, beside her own two.

When all was made ready, and it was getting near to night in the afternoon before Christmas,

Mrs. Livingston sent a messenger for three men from the farm. When they were come, she called in three African servants, and she said to the six men, "Saddle horses and ride away, each one of you in a different direction, and go to every house within five miles of here, and ask: "Are any children in this habitation?" Then say that you are sent to fetch the children's stockings, that Santa Claus wants them, and take special care to bring me *two* stockings from each child, whose father or brother is away fighting for his country."

So the six men set forth on their queer errand, after stockings, and they rode up hill and down, and to the great river's bank, and wherever the message was given at a house door, if a child was within hearing, off flew a stocking, and sometimes two, as the case might be about father and brother.

Now, in a deep little dell, about five miles away, there was a small, old brown house, and in it lived Mixie Brownson with her mother and brother, but this night Mixie was all alone. When one of the six horsemen rode up to the door, and without getting down from his horse, thumped away on it with his riding-whip handle, Mixie thought, "Like as not it is an Indian," but she straightway lifted the wooden latch and opened the door.

"There's one child here, I see," said the black man. "Any more?"

" I'm all alone," trembled forth poor Mixie.

" More's the pity," said the man. " I want one of your stockings; two of 'em, if you're a soldier's little girl. I'm taking stockings to Santa Claus."

"O take both mine, then, please," said Mixie with delight, and she drew off two warm woolen stockings and made them into a little bundle, which he thrust into a bag, and off he rode. Mixie's father was a Royalist, fighting with the Indians for the British, but then Mrs. Livingston knew nothing about that.

It was nearly midnight when the stockings reached Fort Safety. It was in this very room that Mrs. Livingston and Aunt Elise received them. Some were sweet and clean, and some were not; some were new and some were old. So they looked them over, and made two little piles, the one to be filled, the other to be washed.

About this time Santa Claus came down from his locked-up room, with pack after pack, and began to fill stockings. There were ninety-seven of them, beside sixteen more that were hung on a line stretched across the fire-place by the children before they went to bed, so as to be very handy for Santa Claus when he should enter by the chimney.

" What an awful rich lady my fine old Grand-mother Livingston must have been, to have goodies enough to fill 113 stockings!" said Carl, his red hair fairly glistening with interest and pride; while Bessie and Dot looked eagerly at the fire-place **and around** the room, to see if any fragment of **a stocking might, by any** chance, be about anywhere.

Well, at last the stockings were full. I cannot **tell you** exactly **what was** in **them.** I remember that my grandmother said, that in every. stocking went, first of all, a nice, pretty **pair of** new ones, just the size of the old ones ; and **next, a** pair of mittens to fit hands belonging with **feet** that could wear the stockings. I know there **were** oranges and some kind of candy, too.

At last **the** stockings were all hung on a line extending along **two** sides **of the** room, and Mrs. Livingston and **Aunt Elise** locked the room, and **being** very tired, **went to bed. The** next morning, bright **and** early, there was **a great** pattering of bare feet **and a** flitting **of** night-gowns down the staircase, past the evergreen trees **in the** hall, **and a little host** of twelve children stood **at that** door, trying **to get in ;** but it was **all of no use,** and they had to march back to bed again.

As for Otis Grey, he was **a** real Boston boy, full of the spirit of **a** Liberty **Rebel.** He dressed himself slyly, slipped **down on the** great stair-rail, so as **to make no noise,** opened softly the hall-door, **went** outside, climbed up, and looked **into the room.** When he peeped, he was so **frightened at the** long line of fat stockings that he made **haste** down, and **never** said **a** word to anybody, except my grandmother (Lorinda Grey, his **sister) ;** and they two kept the secret.

Breakfast time came, and not a child of the dozen had heard a word from Santa Claus that morning.

Mrs. Livingston said a very long grace, and after that she said to the children : " I have disappointed you this morning, but you will all have your stockings as soon as a little company I have invited to spend the day with you, is come."

" Bless me !" whispered Otis Grey to his sister, are all them stockings a-coming ?"

" Otis," said Mrs. Livingston, "you may leave the table."

Otis obeyed silently, and lost his Christmas breakfast for the time. Mrs. Livingston had strict laws in her house, and punishment always followed disobedience.

The morning was long to the children, but it was a busy time in the winter kitchen, and even the summer kitchen was alive with cookery; and at just midday Philip cried out " Company's come, grandma !"

A dozen or more of the stocking-owners were at the door. In they trooped, bright and laughing and happy. Before they were fairly inside, more came, and more, and still more, until full sixty boys and girls were gathered up and down the great hall and parlors. Mixie Brownson came on the last sled-load. Now Mrs. Livingston did not know, even by name, more than one-half of the young folks she had undertaken to make happy that day; but that made no manner of difference, and the children had not the least idea that Santa Claus had their stockings all hung up in this room, until suddenly the doors were opened, and there was the great hickory-wood fire, and the sunlight streaming in, and the stockings, fat and bulging, hanging in rows. Some were red, and some were blue, and some were white, and some were mixed. Grand old Mrs. Livingston stood within the room, her white curls shining and her stiff brocade trailing.

"Come in, children," she said, and in they trooped, silent with awe and wonder at the sight they saw. The lady arranged them side by side, in lines, on the two sides of the room where the stockings were not, and then she said:

"Santa Claus, come forth!"

In yonder corner there began a motion in the branches of the evergreen tree, and such a Santa Claus as crept forth was never seen before. He was bulgy with furs from crown to foot, but he made a low curve over toward Mrs. Livingston, and then nodded his head about the lines of children.

"Good day to you, this Christmas," he said.

"Wish you Merry Christmas, Santa Claus," said Philip, with a bow.

"Here's business," said Santa Claus. "Stockings, let me see. Whoever owns the stocking that I take down from the line, will step forward and take it."

Every single one of the children knew his or her own property, at a glance. Santa Claus had a busy time of it handing down stockings, and a few minutes later he escaped without notice, and was seen no more that year, in Fort Safety.

After the stockings came dinner, and such a dinner as it was! Whatever there was not, I remember that it was told to me that there was great abundance of English plum-pudding. After dinner came games and more happiness, and after the last game, came time to go home. The sweet clear afternoon suddenly became dark with clouds, and it began to snow soon after the first load set off. One or two followed, and by the time the last one was ready to start, Mrs. Livingston looked forth and said "not another child should leave her roof that night in such a blinding storm."

Eight little hands clapped their new mittens together in token of joy, but poor little Mixie Brownson began to cry. She had never in her life been away from the brown house.

Tea was served, and Mixie was comforted for a short time. After that came games again, until all were weary with play : and Otis Grey begged Mrs. Livingston for a story.

Mixie was tearful still, and she crept shyly to the lady's side and sobbed forth : " I wish you was my grandma and would take me in your lap."

Mrs. Livingston stooped and kissed Mixie's cheek, then lifted her on her knees and began to tell the children a story. It must have been a very pretty picture that the old, blowing snow-

storm looked in upon that night, in this very
room: twenty or more children seated around
the fire-circle, with stately Mrs. Livingston and
pretty Aunt Elise in their midst.

Whilst all this was going on within, outside a
band of Indians, led by a white man, was approaching Fort Safety to burn it down.

Step by step, the savages crept nearer and
nearer, until they were standing in the very light
that streamed out from the Christmas windows.

The white man who led them was in the service of the English, and knew every step of the
way, and just who lived in the great house.

He ordered them to stand back while he
looked in.   Creeping closer and closer, he
climbed, as Otis Grey had done, and put his face
to the window-pane.   He saw Mrs. Livingston
and Miss Elise, and the great circle of eager, interested faces, all looking at the story-teller, and
he wiped his eyes in order to get one more good
look, for he could not believe the story they told
to him: that his own poor little Mixie was in
there, sitting in proud Mrs. Livingston's lap,
looking happier than he had ever seen her.   He
stayed so long, peering in, that the savages grew
impatient.   One or two of their chief men crept
up and put their swarthy faces beside his own.

It so happened that at that moment Aunt Elise
glanced toward the window.   She did not scream,
she uttered no word; but she fell from her chair
to the floor.

"His own poor little Mixie was there, sitting in proud Mrs. Livingston's lap."

Mixie's father, for it was he who led the savages, saw what was happening within, and ordered the Indians to march away and leave the big house unhurt. They grunted and grumbled, and refused to go until they had been told that the little girl on the lady's knee was his little girl.

"He not going to burn his own papoose," explained the Indian chief to his red men ; and then the evil band went groping away through the storm.

The story to the children was not finished that night, for on the floor lay pretty Aunt Elise, as white as white could be ; and it was a long time before she was able to speak. As soon as she could sit up, she wished to get out into the open air.

Mrs. Livingston went with her, and when she was told what had been seen at the window, they together examined the freshly fallen snow and found traces of moccasined feet.

With fear and trembling, the two ladies entered the house. Not a word of what had been seen was spoken to servant or child. Aunt Elise from an upper window kept watch during the time that Mrs. Livingston returned thanks to God for the happy day the children had passed, and asked His love and protecting care during the silent hours of sleep.

Then the sleepy, happy throng climbed the wide staircase to the rooms above, went to bed and slept until morning.

Not a red face approached Fort Safety that night. The two ladies, letting the Christmas fires go down, kept watch from the windows until the day dawned.

"I'm so glad," exclaimed Carl, "that my fine, old, greatest of grandmothers thought of having that good time at Christmas."

"Dear me!" sighed Bessie, "if she hadn't, we wouldn't have this nice home to-day."

"Mamma," said Dot, "let's have a good stocking-time next Christmas; just like that one, all but the Indians."

"O, mamma, *will you?*" cried Bessie, jumping with glee.

"Where *would* we get the soldiers' children, though," questioned Carl.

"Lots of 'em in Russia and Turkey, if we only lived there," observed Bessie. "But there's *always* plenty of children that *want* a good time and never get it, just as much as the soldiers' children did. Will you, mamma?"

"When Christmas comes again, I will try to make just as many little folks happy as I can," said Mrs. Livingston.

"And we'll begin *now*," said Carl, "so as to be all ready. I shall saw all summer, so as to make lots of pretty brackets and things."

"And I s'pose I shall have to dress about five hundred dolls to go 'round," sighed Bessie, "there are so many children now-a-days."

The Old Porter House

A DAY AND A NIGHT IN THE OLD PORTER HOUSE.

MONDAY morning, July 5th, 1779, was oppressively warm and sultry in the Naugatuck Valley. Great Hill, that rises so grandly to the northward of Union City, and at whose base the red house still nestles that was built either by Daniel Porter or his son Thomas before or as early as 1735, was bathed in the full sunlight, for it was past eight of the clock. Up the hill had just passed a herd of cows owned by Mr. Thomas Porter and driven by his son Ethel, a lad of fourteen, and Ethel's sister Polly, aged twelve years.

"It's awful hot to-day!" said Ethel, as he threw himself on the grass at the hill-top—the cows having been duly cared for.

"You'd better not lose time lying here," said Polly. "There's altogether too much going on uptown to-day, and there's lots to do before we go up to celebrate."

"One thing at a time," replied Ethel, "and this is my time to rest. I never knew a hill to grow so much in one night before."

"Well! you can rest, but I'm going to find out what that fellow is riding his poor horse so fast for this hot morning—somebody **must** be dying! Just **see** that line of dust a mile away!" and Polly started down Great Hill to meet the rider.

The horseman stayed his horse at Fulling Mill Brook to give him a drink, and Polly reached the brook just at the instant the **horse buried his nose** in the cool stream.

"Do **you** live near here?" questioned the rider.

"My **father**, Mr. Thomas Porter, keeps the **inn** yonder," said Polly.

"I **can't stop**," said the horseman, "though I've ridden from **New Haven** without breakfast, and I must **get up to the Center; but you** tell your father the *British* are landing at West Haven. They have more that forty vessels! The new president was on the tower of the College when I came by, watching with his spy-glass, and he shouted **down** that he could see them, landing."

At that instant, Ethel reached the **brook**. "What's going on?" he questioned.

"You're a likely looking **boy—you'll do**!" said the horseman, with a glance at Ethel, cutting off at the same instant the **draught** his horse was enjoying, by a sudden **pull at the** bridle lines. "You **go tell the news! Get out** the militia! Don't lose a minute."

"What **news?** What for?" asked Ethel, but the **rider was** flying onward.

"A pretty time we'll have celebrating to-day," said Polly, to herself, dipping the corner of her apron into the brook and wiping her heated face with it, as she hurried to the house. Meanwhile, her brother was running and shouting after the man who had ridden off in such haste.

As Polly entered the house the big brick oven stood wide open, and it was filled to the door with a roaring fire. On the long table stood loaves of bread almost ready for the oven. Her sister Sybil was putting apple pies on the same table. Sybil was a beautiful girl of twenty years, much admired and greatly beloved in the region.

"What is Ethel about so long this morning, that I have his work to do, I wonder!" exclaimed Mr. Thomas Porter, as he lifted himself from the capacious fire-place in which he had been piling birch-wood under the crane—from which hung in a row three big iron pots.

"It is a pretty hot morning, and the sun is powerful on the hill, father," said Mrs. Mehitable Porter in reply—not seeing Polly, who stood panting and glowing with all the importance of having great news to tell.

"Father," cried Polly, "where is Truman and the men? Send 'em! send 'em everywhere!"

"What's the matter? what's the matter, child?" exclaimed Mr. Porter, while his wife and Sybil stood in alarm.

At that instant Ethel sprang in, crying out, "The · militia! The militia! They want the militia."

"What for, and *who* wants the men?" asked his father.

"I don't know. He didn't stop to tell. He said: 'Get out the militia! Don't lose a minute!' and then rode on."

"Father, *I know*," said Polly. "He told *me*. The British ships, more than forty of them, are landing soldiers at New Haven. President Stiles saw them at daybreak from the college tower with his spy-glass."

Before Polly had ceased to speak, Ethel was off. Within the next ten minutes six horses had set forth from the Porter house—each rider for a special destination.

"I'll give the alarm to the Hopkinses," cried back Polly from her pony, as she disappeared in the direction of Hopkins Hill.

"And I'll stir up Deacon Gideon and all the Hotchkisses from the Captain over and down," said ten-year-old Stephen, as he mounted.

"You'd better make sure that Sergeant Calkins and Roswell hear the news. Tell Captain Terrell to get out his Ring-bone company, and don't forget Captain John and Abraham Lewis, Lieutenant Beebe, and all the rest. It isn't much use to go over the river—not much help *we'd* get, however much the British might, on that side," advised Mr. Porter, as the fourth messenger departed.

When the last courier had set forth, leaving only Mr. and Mrs. Porter, Sybil and two servants in the house, Mr. Porter said to his wife: " I believe, mother, that I'll go up town and see what I can do for Colonel Baldwin and Phineas." Major Phineas Porter was his brother, who six months earlier had married Melicent, daughter of Colonel Baldwin and widow of Isaac Booth Lewis (the lady whose name has been chosen for the Waterbury, Connecticut, Chapter of Daughters of the American Revolution).

After Mr. Porter's departure Mrs. Porter said to Sybil, " You remember how it was two years ago at the Danbury alarm, how we were left without a crumb in the house and fairly went hungry to bed. I think I'd better stir up a few extra loaves of rye bread and make some more cake. You'd better call up Phyllis and Nancy and tell them to let the washing go and help me."

Phyllis and Nancy were filled with astonishment and awe at the command to leave the washing and bake, for, during their twenty years' service in the house, nothing had ever been allowed to stay the progress of Monday's washing.

Before mid-day another messenger came tearing up the New Haven road and demanded a fresh horse in order to continue the journey to arouse help and demand haste. He brought the half-past nine news from New Haven that fifteen hundred men were marching from West Haven Green to the bridge, that women and children were escaping to the northward and westward with all the treasure that they could carry, or

13

bury on the way, because every horse in the town had been taken for the defence.

He had not finished his story, when from the northward the hastily equipped militia came hurrying down the road. It was reported that messengers had been posted from Waterbury Centre to Westbury and to Northbury; to West Farms and to Farmingbury—all parts of ancient Waterbury—and soon The City, as it was called in 1779, now Union City, would be filled with militiamen.

The messenger from New Haven grew impatient for the fresh horse he had asked for. While he waited on the porch, Cato, son of Phyllis, whose duty it was to make ready his steed, sought Mrs. Porter in the kitchen.

"Where that New Haven fellow," he asked, "get Massa's horse. He say he come from New Haven, and he got the horse Ethel went away on."

"Are you sure, Cato?"

"Sure's I know Cato," said the boy, "and the horse he knew me—be a fool if he didn't."

Mrs. Porter immediately summoned the rider to her presence and learned from him that about four miles down the road his pony had given out under haste and heat; that he had met a boy who, pitying its condition, had offered an exchange of animals, provided the courier would promise to leave his pony at the Porter Inn and get a fresh horse there.

"Just like Ethel!" said Polly. "He'll dally all day now, while that horse gets rested and fed, or else he'll go on foot. I wonder if I couldn't catch him!"

"Polly," said Mrs. Porter, "don't you leave this house to-day without my permission."

Poor Mrs. Porter! Truman, her eldest son, had gone. He was sixteen and had been a "trained" soldier for more than six months; that, the mother expected; but Ethel, only fourteen, and full of daring and boyish zeal! Stephen also, the youngest, and the baby, being but ten years old—he had not yet returned from "stirring up the Hotchkisses." Had he followed Captain Gideon?

"Ethel is too far ahead," sighed Polly. "I couldn't catch him now, even if mother would let me; but here comes Uncle Phineas in his regimentals, and Aunt Melicent and Polly and little Melicent, and O! what a crowd! I can't see for the dust! It's better than the celebration. It's so *real*, so 'strue as you live and breathe and everything."

Polly ran to the front door. At that day it opened upon a porch that extended across the house front. This porch was supported by a line of white pillars, and a rail along its front had rings inserted in it to which a horseman could, after dismounting beneath its shelter, secure his steed. Long ago, this porch was removed and the house itself was taken from the roadside on the plain below, because of a great freshet, and removed to its present location. The history of that porch, of the men and women who dismounted beneath its shelter, or who, footsore and weary, mounted its steps, would be the history of the country for more than a century, for the men of Waterbury were in every enterprise in which the colonies were engaged ; but this is the record of a single day in its eventful life, and we must return to the porch, where Polly is welcoming Mrs. Melicent Porter with the words: " Mother will be so glad you have come, Aunt Melicent, for Ethel has gone off to New Haven and he's miles ahead of catching, and Stephen hasn't got back yet from 'rousing the Alarm company. Mother wouldn't *say* a word, but she has got her mouth fixed and I know she's afraid he's gone, too. I don't know what father will do when he finds it out."

" You go, now," said Mrs. Porter, "and tell your mother that your father staid to go to the mill. He will not be here for some time."

While Polly went to the kitchen with the message, Mrs. Melicent alighted from her horse and, assisting her little daughter Melicent from the saddle, said : " You are heavier to-day, Milly, than you were when I threw you to the bank from my horse when it was floating down the river. I couldn't do it now."

The instant Major Porter had set little Polly Lewis on the porch Mrs. Porter was beside him, begging that he would look for Ethel and care for the boy if he found him. The promise was given, and looking well despite the uncommon heat, the Major, in all the glory of his military equipment, set forth.

From that moment all was noise and call and confusion without. Men went by singly, in groups, in squads, in companies, mounted and on foot. It is a matter of public record that twelve militia companies, with their respective captains, went from Waterbury alone to assist New Haven in the day of its peril. It is no marvel that they set off with speed, for the horrors of the Danbury burning was yet fresh in memory.

In the long kitchen, as the heated hours went by, the brick oven was fired again and again until the very stones of the chimney expanded with glowing heat, and the last swallow forsook its ancient nest in despair. The sun was in the west when Mr. Porter, with a bag of wheat on one side of the saddle and a bag of rye on the other, appeared at the kitchen entrance and summoned help to unload, but his accustomed helpers were gone. , Even Cato, the reliable, was missing. Phyllis and Nancy received the wheat and the rye.

"Mother," said Mr. Porter, "I had to do the grinding myself—couldn't find a man to do it, and I knew it couldn't be done here to-day, water's too low. Where are the boys?" he questioned, as he entered and looked around. When informed, his sole ejaculation was, "I ought to have known that boys always have gone and always will go after soldiers."

"Don't worry, mother," he added to his wife, as she stood looking wistfully down the road.

There were tears in her eyes as she said: "Not a boy left."

"Why yes, mother, here comes Stephen and Stiles Hotchkiss up the road. My! how tired and hot the boys and the horses do look!" exclaimed Polly.

Stephen waited for no reprimand. He forestalled it by saying: "Captain Hotchkiss let Stiles and me go far enough to *see* the British troops—way off, ever so far—but we saw 'em, we did, didn't we, Stiles?"

"Come! come!" said Mr. Porter, while the lad's mother stood with her hand on his head. "Stephen, tell us all about it!"

"Captain Hotchkiss said he was a boy once, and if we'd promise him to go home the minute he told us to, he'd take us along. Well! we kept meeting folks running away from New Haven, with everything on 'em but their heads. One woman was lugging a lot of salt pork, 'because she couldn't bear to have the Britishers eat it all up;' and another woman was carrying away a lot of candles hanging by a string, and the sun had melted the last drop of tallow, leaving the wicks dangling against the tallow on her dress, but she didn't know it; and mother, would you believe it—Mr. Timothy Atwater told Captain Hotchkiss that he met a woman whom he knew hurrying out of town with a cat in her arms. When he asked her where her children were, she said, 'Why, at home I suppose.' 'Well,' said Mr. Atwater, 'hadn't you better leave the cat and go back and get them?' And she said, 'Perhaps she had,' and went back for 'em."

"What became of the cat?" asked Mrs. Melicent Porter.

"Why, Aunt Melicent, how nice!" cried Stephen, running back to the porch and returning with a cat in his arms.

"I've fetched her to you. I *knew* you loved cats so! Here she is, black as ink, and she stuck to the saddle every step of the way like a true soldier's cat. I was afraid she'd run away when I took her off the saddle, and I hid her. You know mother don't like cats around under her feet."

In a minute pussy was on the floor, and the last drop of milk in the house was set before her by little Polly Lewis. Little Melicent cooed softly to her, while Stephen and Stiles went on with their story,—from which it was learned that the boys had gone within a mile of Hotchkisstown (now Westville), where, from a height, they had a view of the British troops. The lads were filled with admiration of the marching, "as though it was all one motion," of the "mingling colors of the uniforms worn, as the bright red of the English Foot Guards blended with the graver hues of the dress worn by the German merce- naries," and of "the waving line of glittering bayonets."

"We didn't see," said Stephen, "but just one flash of musketry, because Stiles's father said we must start that instant for home, and he told Stiles to stay here until morning, and we haven't had a mouthful to eat since breakfast, and its been the hottest day that ever was, and I'm tired to death."

"And the cows are on the hill and nobody here to fetch them down," sighed Mr. Porter.

"Such a lot of captains waiting to see you, father!" announced Polly. "There's Captain Woodruff and Captain Castle and Captain Rich- ards and a Fenn captain and a Garnsey captain. I forget the rest." The captains invaded the kitchen itself, declaring that it being Monday in the week, every householder had been short of provisions for the emergency—that every inn on the way and many a private house had been unable to provide enough for so many men, and what could they have at the Porter Inn?

Polly disappeared. Before her father had con- sidered the matter she had, assisted by her Aunt Melicent and Polly Lewis, seized from the pantry shelves all that they could carry, and going by a rear way, had hidden on the garret stairs a big roast of veal, one of lamb, and enough bread and pies for family requirements, and still the pantry shelves seemed amply filled. "I'm not going to have Ethel come home in the night and find nothing left for him I know, and the hungry boys fast asleep and tired out on the kitchen settle will come to life ravenous. Wonder if I hadn't better be missing just now and go fetch the cows down. Father would have asthma all night if he tried it," said Polly to her aunt; and up the hill Polly went accompanied by little Polly—while Mrs. Porter stood by and saw the fruits of her hard day's work vanish out of sight.

"Pray leave something for your own household," she ventured to intercede at last. "Don't forget that we have four guests of our own for the night;" but Mr. Porter, rather proud to show that, however remiss others had been, the Porter Inn was prepared for emergencies, had already bidden Nancy and Phyllis fetch forth the last loaf."

"Like one for supper," ventured Nancy, as her master carefully examined the empty larder, hoping to find something more. As the last captain from Northbury started on the night journey for New Haven, Mr. Porter faced his wife. "Now Thomas Porter," she said, "you can go hungry to bed, but what can I do for my guests and the children and the rest of the household?"

Mr. Porter scratched his head—a habit when profoundly in doubt—and said: "I must fetch the cows! It's most dark now," and set forth, to find that Polly had them all safely in the cattle yard.

"I suppose, father," said Polly, "that we've got to live on milk to-night. I thought so when I heard you parleying with the captains. So I thought I'd get the cows down." As Polly entered the house, she saw a lady and two girls of about her own age, to whom her mother was saying: "We will give you shelter, gladly, but my husband has just let the militia you met just below have the last morsel of cooked food in our house, and we've nothing left for ourselves but milk for supper."

"Mother," said Polly, stepping to the front; "we have plenty! I looked out for you before father got to the pantry. I made journeys to the garret stairs, several of them, and Aunt Melicent and Polly Lewis helped me. It is all right for the lady to stay."

The lady in question was Mrs. Thankful Punderson and her twin daughters, girls of twelve years, who had escaped from New Haven just as the British troops reached Broadway, and the riot and plunder and killing began. "I hoped," she said, "to reach the house of my husband's sister, Mrs. Zachariah Thompson, in Westbury, but Anna and Thankful are too tired to walk further to-night, and the horse can carry but two. It is getting late, and I am so thankful to stay."

As Mr. Porter stood on the porch looking down the road for the next arrival, hoping to learn some later news and perhaps to hear Ethel's cheery call in the distance, Polly said: " Father, will you let me be innkeeper to-night? "

" Gladly, Polly, with nothing to keep and not a room to spare," was his reply.

" Then I'll invite you to supper, and mind, if the ministers themselves come, they can't have a bite to-night, for I'm the keeper."

" I suppose you've made us some hasty pudding while the milking was going on," he said, as Polly, preceding her father for once, went before, and opened the door upon a table abundantly supplied, and laid for twelve.

At the table Mr. Porter told, for the benefit of Mrs. Melicent Porter and Mrs. Punderson, some of the events, both pathetic and tragic, that had occurred in the old house during his boyhood and youth, and Mrs. Melicent Porter told again the events of the day in June—only a year before —wherein the battle of Monmouth had been fought near her New Jersey home, and she had spent the day in doing what she could to relieve the sufferings of men so spent with battle and heat and wounds that they panted to her door with tongues hanging from their mouths; also of her perilous journey from New Jersey to Connecticut on horseback, accompanied by Lieutenant-Colonel Baldwin, her father—during which journey it was, that she had thrown her daughter Melicent in safety from her horse to the bank of the river they were fording, while the animal, having lost its footing, was going down the current.

While these things had been in the telling, Polly had slipped from the table unnoticed, and had lighted every lamp that could brighten the house front and serve to guide to its porch. The last lamp was just alight when Polly's guests began to arrive. She half expected soldiers, and refugees came. It seemed to her that every family in New Haven must be related to every family in Waterbury—so many women and children came in to rest themselves before continuing the journey and "to wait until the moon should rise," for the evening was very dark, and oh! the stories that each fresh arrival brought! They filled the group that came in to listen with fear and agony. New Haven was very near to Waterbury in that day. The inhabitants there were closely connected with the inhabitants here, and their peril and distress was a common woe. Little Stiles Hotchkiss cried himself to sleep that night, fearing that one of the three Hotchkisses, reported killed, might be his father.

Polly acted well her part. To the children she gave fresh milk; to their elders she explained that the militia had taken their supplies, while she made place to receive two or three invalids who could go no further, by giving up her own room.

"You'll let me lie on the floor in your room, Aunt Melicent, I know," she said, "for the poor lady is so old and so feeble; I'm most sure she is a hundred. She came in a chaise and wanted to get up to Parson Leavenworth's, but she just can't. She can't hold up her head."

It was near midnight when the refugees set forth for the Center, Mr. Porter himself acting as guide. After that time, the sleepy boys and the entire household having taken themselves to bed, the old house was left to the night, with its silence and its chill dampness that always comes up from the river, that goes on "singing to us the same bonny nonsense," despite our cheer or our sorrow. Again, and yet again through the night, doors opened and two mothers stepped out in the moonlight to listen, hoping—hoping to hear sound of the coming of the boys, but only the lone cry of the whippoorwill was borne on the air.

"'Pears like," said Phyllis to Mrs. Porter in the morning, "the whippoorwills had lots to say last night; talked all night so's you couldn't hear nothing 'tall."

"Phyllis," said Mrs. Porter, "there was nothing else to hear, but we shall know soon."

Polly came down, bringing her checked linen apron full of eggs for breakfast. "I thought, mother," she said, "that you'd leave yourself without an egg yesterday, so I looked out. Isn't it handy to have them in the house? Haven't heard a single cackle this morning yet, but yesterday was a remarkable day everyway. I believe the hens knew the British were coming. Did you ever see such eggs? Wonder if my old lady is awake yet! Guess I'll carry up some hot water for her and find out."

Polly poured the water deftly from the big iron tea-kettle hanging from the crane and hurried away with it, only to return with such haste that she tripped on the threshold, broke the pitcher and sent the water over everything it could reach. " Mother," she said, recovering herself, " Parson Leavenworth will be here to breakfast. He's coming down the road with father. My old lady will feel honored, won't she? I know he's come for her. Phyllis, any more hot water to spare? It's so good to take out wrinkles; she'll miss it, I know."

The sun had not climbed over Great Hill when breakfast was over, and the last guest of the night had gone. Mrs. Punderson's daughter Anna rode behind the Rev. Mark Leavenworth on his horse, Thankful with Mrs. Punderson, the old lady in the chaise, and even Stiles had galloped away toward the east, and yet not a traveler on the road had brought tidings from New Haven. The group on the porch watching the departure had not dispersed when Polly's ears caught a strain floating up the river valley. She listened. She ran. She clasped her mother in her arms. She kissed her. She whispered in her ear, " I hear him! He's coming! Ethel is; and Cato is with him!" she cried out, embracing Phyllis in her joy. The two mothers—the one white, the other black; the one free, the other in bonds—went to listen. They stood side by side on the porch ; tears fell from their eyes, tears that

through all the years science has failed to distin-
guish, the one from the other. Ethel's cheery
call rang clear and clearer. Cato's wild cadence
grew near and nearer, but when the boys rode up
beside the porch, Mrs. Porter was on her knees in
the little bed-room off the parlor, and Phyllis was
in the kitchen. New England mothers, both of
them! Their sorrows they could bear; their joys
they hid from sight.

WATERBURY, CONN.,
   September, 1898.